Secret in the
Stlalakum Wild

Secret in the Stlalakum Wild

Christie Harris
Illustrated by Douglas Tait

Atheneum 1972 New York

To the long-gone old-timers
who first told me about stlalakums
Cornelius Kelleher
and
Mrs. Fraser York

1996 4

Secret in the Stlalakum Wild

1

THE WOLF STILL HOWLS, LONG AND LONE, IN OUR continent's northwest. The coast is still lonely. And the wild westerlies sweep in with the scream of the sea birds.

Mazes of islands confuse the way into the dark, heavily timbered mountains that drop down to the ocean. Then thick underbrush further slows the intruder. Muskegs trap the unwary like quicksands. And deep mosses muffle the shouts of the alien who has lost his way.

The deep mosses may also muffle the movements of the unnatural beings who, it is whispered, still live in the wildernesses.

Between the secretive trees and the towns is the edge of the forest, where the two meet. And it is here that the sensitive sometimes catch their breath, aware of *something*. The solitary hiker or hunter glimpses the hairy, nine-foot sasquatch and wonders if he saw a bear or an almost-man. The bird watcher on a wild cliff catches the alarming undulations of the sea serpent, or the slither of a giant snake through a shadowed, loon-haunted lake that some say is connected with the open sea by a subterranean channel.

Newspaper headlines revive old mysteries: HUNTER FINDS GIANT'S FOOTPRINTS? SEA SERPENT SIGHTED? LAKE MONSTER HERE?

The timid gasp and edge away from the silent forest, away from the lonely waters. For there *is* something strange about the northwest wildernesses.

Bolder with distance, far-off adventurers plan another expedition, hoping that this time they won't be plagued by weird misadventures in those fiercely forbidding mountains, hoping that this time they can persuade some Indian guide to venture into those wildernesses.

Only the old, old Indian murmers "Stlalakum" in a voice that hushes his household. And the word seldom reaches beyond his household. For the Indians are shy with their beliefs. They are reluctant to talk of their pretty young women who have been snatched up by a sasquatch while out picking berries. The young ones are embarrassed about old-fashioned things like forest giants and picking berries; while the old ones have learned that the less you tell white men the better.

Insensitive men who crash through the fragile, living wilderness would never understand about stlalakums. So the Indians keep their silence.

But their silence is vibrant with understanding of the unnatural beings who still live in the natural world here, in these last hiding places. Here, in the few fortresses still standing against the onslaught of the arrogant Tamers of the Wild.

2

LIFE SEEMED ONLY TOO PREDICTABLE TO MORANN ON the blistering hot day her father's sister Sarah was due to arrive. So much so that she took steps to start things off in a new direction. Determined to be somebody's favorite for a change, she went at the day head on. She brushed her hair hard, and she reeked of perfume when she finally emerged from the bathroom.

"P-ew!" her slightly plump, slightly older sister Robin observed at the breakfast table. "Who are you trying to impress?"

"*Nosey* people," Morann answered. But she smiled. She was not going to rise to anyone's bait this morning. Aunt Sarah probably liked girls who fought only for Peace. So she practiced feeling like a butterfly flitting about among daisies.

Sarah was a university student. And she was coming to do something "meaningful yet restful" for two weeks before she started a summer course.

"Meaningful, maybe," Dad had remarked when her letter arrived. "But restful?"

Morann knew what he meant. And now she frowned at Robin and Kath and little Gregory. The other kids in this family were not exactly butterflies flitting silently among daisies.

"Get on with your egg, Morann!" Kath ordered. "Then hit the bedrooms!" Kath was the tallest, oldest, darkest, skinniest, and bossiest of the Fenn girls.

"You're not the boss of me," Morann retorted before she remembered her sweetness and light.

"I'll clean the car," Robin announced. She always got to do the outdoor jobs since she made a career of being like a boy.

"And I'll do the dishes," Kath said. Her tone indicated that this was no time to have a wrecking crew in the kitchen. It also suggested that the oldest girl had to be extremely long-suffering.

Morann just barely stuck her tongue out before smiling down at her little brother. "Gwuggelly, you and me'll do the upstairs."

Gregory could pronounce his name correctly

by this time, but his sisters clung to the nickname he had come up with when he had first tried to say Gregory.

"He used to have trouble with his gwuggle-ues," Morann planned to explain to Aunt Sarah. Actually it was his *r*'s that he had had trouble with. But the gwuggle-ue bit always got a laugh.

It was with a little shiver of excitement that Morann thought about Sarah and her coming visit. For Sarah's idea of a "meaningful" vacation had come out of some newspaper clippings they had sent her, clippings about a sasquatch. Sarah was actually going to an old Indian village to try to find out about strange Indian beliefs.

As she went upstairs, Morann wondered. Would they discover that there really were hairy giants right out in those mountains you could see from the front bedroom window? She looked at the mountains again with fresh interest. They were certainly rugged and wild enough. And people said that Indians wouldn't go into them no matter how much pay they were offered.

"Hit those bedrooms!" Kath ordered from downstairs. Obviously she had heard the climb up the stairs, then only the silence of gazing out a window. Kath had ears like a bugged room.

Morann stuck her tongue out in the direction of the kitchen. "Gwuggelly, you get over on that side of the bed. We'll just kind of wave the covers and pull them up." Kath was safely down-

stairs. Robin was safely in the driveway. And Mom was on the phone, checking flight arrival time. So Morann could do her work her way, for once.

But Gregory sat down on the floor and began to giggle.

"Oh, no!" Morann begged him. "Not Mousie now!"

He shook his left foot, laughing. "Mousie's tickling me," he reported.

"But—"

But you couldn't tell Gregory there was nothing in his shoe except his foot, and maybe a case of pins and needles. He had an awful imagination. Mom sometimes looked anxious about him. She was sure he wasn't relating to reality. Yet she didn't want to *trauma* him. She said maybe Gregory was going to be very creative. But she still looked worried, even when Neil next door said the only thing wrong with the kid was too many fool sisters.

"Come on, Gregory!" Morann commanded, picking up one corner of the covers to begin the waving operation. "We've got to go to the airport."

It was a terribly hot day to go anywhere. No one was really used to heat in the northwest. And since Dad had gone north on one of his geology jobs, Mom was in charge of transportation. She had run the car out in the sun for Robin to clean it. Robin, of course, had shut all the windows so she could really have fun with the hose. And then, when Sarah's flight was delayed, everybody forgot about moving the car. So it was like an oven when they were finally ready to leave.

"It's hot, and it's going to get hotter," Mom cautioned them, blocking the scramble for what shade there was in the car. "So don't jostle and fight. Just stay quiet!"

"I've taken my pill," Kath reported. And looking suitably wan, she got into the back seat and leaned into the corner that was going to be on the shady side going in. With her threat of carsickness, Kath always had her pick of seats.

"I'll navigate," Robin said, grabbing the shaded front seat. "It's tricky getting into that airport."

"It's tricky getting into that front seat," Morann mumbled. She always got elbowed out of the way when there were signs to watch for, or a map to read. But she was not going to fight for her rights today. She'd only end up sweaty and mad and not Aunt Sarah's favorite.

But it was murder on the sunny side of the car. When you held up a map for shade, your arms ached. When you just turned your back on the sun, you barbecued. Morann's clothes were sticking to her long before they reached the airport. And, feeling madder by the mile, she glared across Gregory at her older sister.

Kath was busy with her notebook, keeping track of how many campers they passed, or what percentage of the cars pulled trailers, or something. She just loved to announce suddenly a fact like four percent of the cars kept their lights on in the daytime.

Morann squashed her mouth shut. Just because Kath had once been carsick, she had a corner on the best seat for life. And because she was Kath, nobody had ever called her bluff. Maybe it was about time somebody did.

The idea was in action before Morann could think about it.

"I feel queasy," she announced. She made a queasy face and grabbed at her throat. "I feel sick," she announced in a suitably blunt wail.

"You do not," Kath snapped at her, coming up out of her statistics to protect her status as the only member of the family who got carsick.

"I do so." Morann glared straight back. "I'm going to be sick."

"Not in the car!" Mom begged, swerving to the side of the road and pulling up in a series of jerks that would not have done much for a genuine case of carsickness. "Open all the windows! Kath, let Morann sit in the shade. And hurry!"

"But Mom!" Kath let go with one huge protest before flinging herself across Gregory; while Morann sprinted guiltily round the back of the car to the shady side. Then they both leaned back, looking as wan as you can look with defiant, hot, pink faces.

"Carsick!" Kath scoffed as they moved off in a series of jerks. "Humbug!"

"You ought to know," Morann shot back.

Robin ignored the battle. With her maps spread out, she was safe in the shaded front seat. And anyway, Morann thought grimly, Robin wasn't ever likely to need carsickness. She had her thing, the thing that made her different. She was a roaring tomboy. She always acted as if she had been named after an ancestor called Robin Hood and so could be expected to drop down out of trees onto unexpecting people. Though Neil next door said the reason her name suited her was that robins liked nothing better than fighting and also ate six times their own weight daily. He was one of the people she liked to drop down onto, or grab and wrestle. And privately Morann predicted that one day, when he got big enough to do it, Neil was going to slaughter Robin.

Morann glanced over at Kath, who was sitting in the sun grabbing at her throat as if trouble was coming right up. Why did she have to be so fierce about it? When she didn't even need the distinction of carsickness. Kath was the oldest. She could make better pies than Mom and sew costumes without help. She was always president or pianist or something. Why couldn't Kath be satisfied with praise, straight A's, no hand-me-downs, and Neil liking her gingerbread? Why did she have to be carsick, too?

Only Gregory had it better than Kath. He could have settled for just being the youngest, for just being cute. But like Kath, he was born lucky. In fact, he was even luckier than she was. For his thing got nothing but affection and gales of laughter.

"Morann," he said now, as though by way of airing his thing. He pointed to a steamship company's billboard. "Morann, do you think . . . maybe . . . maybe ships have feet away down there under the water? Like ducks. And maybe they're swimming. Do you? Maybe?"

Kath grabbed the question. "Of course we do, honey," she said, beating Morann to the doting big sister act.

Gregory's thing was his wild imagination.

Morann clamped her teeth shut. Gregory would

captivate Sarah without even trying. Everyone loved him on sight. He had it made. Everybody had it made. Everybody else. And it wasn't fair. "Ships swimming!" she scoffed. "Anybody with half a brain knows that ships have engines, like cars."

"You ought to know about anybody with half a brain," Kath said. "Don't mind, her, Gwuggelly. Morann doesn't know much."

"I know one thing. It's hot as hell."

"Morann!" Mom was shocked.

Robin turned her head and grinned at her sister. "Then you'd better grab the chance to get acclimatized."

Morann blasted her breath out. She felt more like a snorting bull than a butterfly. But she was not going to say one more word. She blinked hard, watching out the window.

She was still sitting there, mute with martyrdom, when Mom said, "Thank goodness, here's the airport. And don't any of you dare to start fighting in front of Sarah. She'll think you're a bunch of savages."

Somehow, everyone got out ahead of Morann. Somehow, everyone got in front of her, blocking her off after they spotted Sarah. She knew she wouldn't even be noticed, as usual. Unless . . .

One of her brash comments just seemed to shout itself. "Hey! She's a hippie." Her tone made a hippie something you would hold off until you fixed the clothespin on your nose.

"Morann!" Mom glared at her, as usual.

"Hi," Sarah greeted them casually. Actually she looked shining clean in jeans, shirt, sandals, knapsack and very long red hair. Sarah was a lot younger than Mom.

"Don't mind my monsters!" Mom implored in that high voice she got when she was flustered. Her obvious horror of the word "hippie" made it worse than Morann had made it. "Sarah, it's wonderful to see you. And here are the monsters."

"Hi, kids." Sarah's wide smile took them all in.

Morann liked her. And she just terribly wished that the liking could go two ways. Why did she always blurt out something stupid when she desperately wanted to say something nice? Somehow, what she said never came out cute or smart, it just seemed to come out loud.

Keeping up a bold front, Morann cringed inwardly. She had panicked, as usual. But what were you going to do if you hadn't been born with something that just naturally made you noticeable?

Sunk in despair, she kept her mouth shut most of the way home.

The others jabbered, plying Sarah with questions about what she was going to do. And Kath, of course, made neat notes about the subject: *Indian. Supernatural. River devil in canyon. Sas-*

quatch in mts. Lake serpent. Sea serpent. She was so quick at jotting notes she'd probably get to go everywhere with Sarah, like a secretary.

Morann blurted out a countersuggestion. "Gwuggelly's the one you ought to take into the woods with you, Sarah. He can see invisible things."

"Like Mousie," the others agreed, laughing.

"I can so see Mousie," Gregory piped up.

"Of course you can, honey," Kath soothed him. She was forgetting to look wan. Or perhaps she had realized that carsickness would not exactly qualify her for getting to go with Sarah.

"I know he can see Mousie," Morann admitted; and she wished her admission hadn't come out bristling like a hedgehog. Actually, she had long ago decided that Gregory was on the level. In fact, his invisible friends bothered her a little on dark nights.

"Anybody could see a sasquatch," Robin pointed out. Anybody who could climb a tree, she meant, anybody who could drop down onto one with a rope net.

There it was, Morann told herself. Everybody would get to go except her. They'd say her loudness would scare the sasquatch off or something.

"I'm not really planning a safari into the mountains," Sarah told them. "I'm merely exploring the possibility of doing some real research next year. Actually, I'm hoping to find out a lot by just

· 16 ·

talking to the old Indians along the river."

"Then don't take Morann with you," Kath cautioned, only half joking. "She'd bellow, 'Do you scalp people?' and put them right off."

"I would not!"

"Girls!" Mom's voice was really high-pitched this time. "If Sarah's smart, she won't take any of you."

Morann looked out the window, blinking hard. Aunt Sarah's favorite? She just wished she hadn't got up so early and stunk herself up with that damn perfume.

3

DAD PHONED HOME TO SAY HELLO TO SARAH, AND to tell her he might not get back until the night before she was leaving.

Two days later, Sarah went off to talk to the old Indians along the river. She took Kath and Robin with her, naturally. Robin could navigate. Kath could take notes when they got there.

Morann was left at home, like Gregory. And with the heat wave still on, she loafed around in the shade, where at least she'd be handy if Neil ever stopped weeding the garden next door. She had a huge jug of lemonade, just in case he got thirsty. And when she finally read Gregory a story, she read it loud enough for someone about twenty-five yards away to hear.

"Do you think Gregory's deaf?" Neil asked, jumping the fence when she had finished off *The Three Bears.* "Or were you just born loud?"

Morann poured out a glass of lemonade and took the lid off the can of cookies. "Kath baked them. Molasses," she whispered.

Neil took three and ate them with his usual attention to Kath's masterpieces. Then he said, "I've got problems."

"Even when Robin's not here?"

"I don't suppose you have any money."

"Then you suppose wrong." Morann snapped off her belt purse triumphantly and dumped her fortune out onto the book: one dime, two nickels, and three pennies.

Neil flicked a glance at them. "Guess I'll have to tap Angus." His friend Angus was even keener than Neil was on producing scientific stinks; but Angus had money to support his experiments. "I need some equipment."

Morann picked up her coins, wishing she hadn't wasted her money on perfume. It would have been very satisfying to come to Neil's rescue. "What are you going to blow up this time?" she asked with real interest and a nod towards his basement workshop.

"Well. . . ." He hedged for a moment. Then, overcome by his own enthusiasm, he said, "I'll show you something," and darted off.

He came back with a battered old copy of *Wildlife*. "Picked this up at the dump," he said, opening it eagerly to a double-page picture of a man and a big, potted plant. "Look at that!"

"I'm looking." But it was just a man operating a sort of telegraph key; and he had something wired to a big, heart-shaped green leaf.

"A lie detector," Neil explained. "That's Cleve Backster and his polygraph. He's a scientist who teaches intelligence agents how to record a suspect's emotional reaction to questions. You know. They ask a suspect a question. And his emotional responses make jiggly lines on a strip of paper." He traced the jagged line running down a strip of cross-lined paper at the edge of the picture. "You know. A psychogalvanic reflex reading. A PGR."

"Oh sure. A PGR," Morann said, as if she had heard it lots of times. "So what's the plant suspected of? Murder? Where were you, plant, on the night of—"

"Shut up!" Neil's eyes were bright with excitement. "He discovered that plants react like people. They get all excited when you just even think of hurting them. And it doesn't matter how far away you are when you do the thinking." Neil turned the page to show her the sharp jog in the line where it said "First thought about burning leaf." He pointed to the equally startled jog where it said "Left test lab to look for a match."

"You mean—a plant winces?"

"Plants," Neil informed her, "appear to react emotionally to every threat to their well-being. They even react to every threat to the well-being of any other bundle of living cells." He pointed now to a lesser jog where it said "Shrimp dropped and killed."

"Leaping leppercorns!"

"But," Neil said, looking at her and not the magazine, "plants have nothing to think with or feel with."

"But if they do, then they have."

Neil ignored her logic. "It must be some kind of vibrations. Some natural law of communications that nobody's thought of yet. Living cells—in you, in the plant, in the dog—must send out signals; and the signals can go hundreds of miles, leaping over anything, flashing through anything. It's a whole new thing."

"It's a whole new worry." The times she had just walked along with a stick, walloping the tops off grass and the ends off branches! "Neil, if plants wince, they *must* feel things and think about things." And hate you. And send out bad signals about you.

"But they've got nothing to feel with or think with, I told you."

"But how do you know?" It was creepy to think that everything around you was silently screaming at you. "I'll never pull out weeds

again," she declared. "And I sure won't push the lawnmower."

"You never do push the lawnmower," Neil pointed out.

"Maybe not. But now I have a reason. Poor little leaves!"

Then a happier thought struck her. For once in her life, she was going to impress the others with her superior knowledge. Maybe even Sarah didn't know about this.

With a new object in mind, Morann pumped Neil for information. She felt a small twinge of guilt about his surprised respect for her interest in science. But that interest deepened as she read the *Wildlife* article, skipping over words like polygraph and psychogalvanic reflexes. She read bits out to Gregory: " 'At that point I blew a cloud of cigarette smoke over the plant without warning, and it produced a jagged little graph . . . which I proclaimed to be a reaction of annoyance.' Wow!"

She asked Neil a few more questions when she took the magazine back. And standing there, trying to follow his answers, she absent-mindedly pulled a leaf off a rosebush and began tearing it apart. "Oh! Excuse me!" she gasped to the rosebush. And she meant it. She could just *feel* the other leaves' horror at what she had done.

Gregory was tagging along, listening wide-eyed but saying nothing. And when they got back to their own yard, she explained the whole thing to him, mainly to practice the little speech she was going to make at dinner.

"Gregory, did you know that plants act like criminals? I mean like people? They wince even when you just think about hurting them, or even when you drop a shrimp and kill it."

She started listening for the car hours before it was due back. And her eyes kept moving over the shade trees. What were all those leaves thinking?

When the car finally did arrive, Kath and Robin burst out of it in the way that had made Neil dub the Fenn girls "The Three Squeals." And there was simply no use trying to say anything sensible until they settled down to supper in the back garden. They often ate there, especially when Dad was away.

Then her chance came. "Uh . . . I don't know if I want to eat this lettuce," Morann said, by way of bringing up the subject.

"Either eat it or keep quiet about it!" Mom ordered.

"Even if it winces?" Gregory asked her.

"Winces?" You could see Mom wondering if she had washed all the worms out.

Kath came closer. "Honey, lettuce doesn't care if you eat it."

"Maybe it does," Morann challenged.

"Maybe it does," Gregory echoed.

"*What* have you been telling that child?" Mom demanded of Morann.

"It's all in Neil's *Wildlife*." Morann knew her voice was defensive, as usual, and loud. But it was so infuriating, the way things always turned out. "A scientist rigged up a plant with a police lie detector; and he got jiggly lines just like a criminal. So there!"

"We'll check with Neil's *Wildlife*," Kath said to everyone in general and to Sarah in particular.

"Okay. Check. And you'll find out that plants do feel."

"Well, so do I," said Robin. "Right now I feel hungry. So it's me or the lettuce. Pardon me, lettuce!" She started to eat her salad with such enthusiasm that the others laughed and followed her lead. And Morann's leaves were lost under more important matters. For Kath began to talk eagerly about sasquatches, two-headed snakes, and other more obscure things.

"What was that word, Kath?" Sarah asked.

"*Stlalakum*," Kath informed her, checking neat notes. "*Anything uncanny is stlalakum. The place. The thing. Stlalakums are unnatural beings living in the natural world.*"

"But, boy! Do they keep stlalakums under wraps!" Robin added.

"We found out there's a Stlalakum Lake up on top of Devil Mountain," Sarah told Mom. "Where the medicine men used to go to get spirit power."

"But it was like prying an oyster open, trying to find out about it," Robin went on. "They guessed maybe people called it Smith Lake now. When are we going there, Sarah?"

"Well . . ." Sarah hedged. "We'll see how the time goes. And the weather."

"Stlalakum," Kath said thoughtfully. "I guess ghosts would be stlalakum."

Mom frowned, nodding towards Gregory.

But Gregory just looked as wide-eyed and interested as ever.

Later, when he was supposed to be asleep upstairs, he called out to Morann from his bedroom window.

"What's on your mind?" she asked as she went into the room he shared with her. But she didn't need to ask. His eyes were fixed on the squirrel picture. And he was moving from place to place, looking at it.

"He's watching me," he told her.

"He can't watch you, Gregory. He's not real."

"But his eyes follow me. He's just waiting till I'm asleep so he can go away again."

"Gregory, he doesn't go away at night and come back before morning."

"Maybe he does." His eyes widened. "I got a idea. Maybe he's skalakum."

"Oh, no!" Morann said, collapsing onto her bed.

"Like ghosts."

"Gregory, there are no ghosts."

"How do you know?"

"Well . . ." Yeah. How did she know? "Look, I'm kind of tired. You go to bed, and I'll just lie here."

"Will you watch the squirrel?"

"Yeah, I'll watch the squirrel. And if I catch him going off, I'll take him by the left leg and throw him down the stairs."

Later, when she was really in bed, Morann found herself sneaking looks at that silly squirrel. In the semidarkness, he did look as if he had his eye on her, watching for her to doze off. And after that leaf thing, what could you be sure of?

Morann just did not seem able to go to sleep. And when she finally did, Neil's dog woke her up, howling that high, scary wail that people said meant the dog could hear a ghost. Maybe he could, she thought with a start, if plants could hear you think. Neil believed they could, and Neil was as sensible as a toothbrush.

Neil's dog howled again, high and long. And Morann wished Gregory would wake up scared and want to climb in with her.

He howled a third time. "Ah-wooooooooooooo!"

She'd wake Gregory up. He had to know about reality, didn't he? "Gregory, wake up!" She slipped over and shook him.

"Hm?" He sat up.

"Gregory, look at your squirrel! It's the middle

· 27 ·

of the night and he's there, isn't he? I've been awake all night, and he hasn't moved an inch. He's just a picture, and he doesn't move."

Gregory looked at the squirrel. He lay down. Closed his eyes. And was fast asleep again.

"Well!" If he wasn't going to even try to learn about reality!

A sudden thought made Morann reverse the custom and climb in with him. How could you know what was real? If plants were sitting there, listening to you, tuning in even on what you were thinking, then maybe ghosts . . .

She pulled the covers up over her head.

4

SARAH WAS UP AT SIX.

"Hi, girls!" she called softly from the hallway. "What do you say we try for Stlalakum Lake today?"

"Yippee!" yelled Robin, rousing the whole household.

Wild with hope, Morann joined the rush to the kitchen.

The sun was streaming in with the promise of a lovely day. And in the trees outside the kitchen window, the birds were getting it underway with chirping and twittering.

As organized as the birds and almost as quick

in her movements, Kath consulted her notes: *"Stlalakum Lake. Top of Devil Mt. Indians afraid of big two-headed snake. Only medicine men dared go. To get more power. And maybe sometimes certain children."*

"Power!" Robin gloated, flexing her muscles. "That's for me."

"Not that kind of power, birdbrain," Kath said. "Sarah, what about sandwiches?"

"Light as possible," Sarah decreed. "Save the weight for the thirst quenchers. It could be hot. And it may be hard going. Nobody seems to think there's a proper trail up to the lake. So we'll take a compass."

"Yippee!" Robin squealed, knowing that she would be going.

Almost holding her breath, Morann got the bread out while Kath darted off to wash. Surely they'd take her this time!

She saw Sarah glance at her, and she caught the doubt in the glance. She caught the touch of reluctance in Sarah's, "I wonder if . . ."

So she jumped at the chance to go. "Do we run up? Or just jog?" Then she waited, desperately wishing the "just jog" hadn't come out so smart alecky.

"I sort of need Morann today," Mom cut in, to get her guest off the hook. "It's very kind of you to take two of the children."

"Children?" Robin protested.

Morann slipped out of the room before anyone saw her eyes. And she stayed out in the garden, apparently absorbed in finding the pearl beads she had lost when she had broken her string a week earlier. Mom was sure she would do something silly and showoff on the mountain—break a leg or be a nuisance or something.

"Good snake hunting!" Morann called when the adventurers poked their heads out of the back door to say good-bye to her. Then she pitched a pearl bead hard against the picnic table.

A few minutes later she heard the phone ring.

"Morann," Mom wailed at her from the back porch. "I'd clean forgotten about this being the day the church women are canning the mince meat for the Fund. Ella's coming by to pick me up at eight o'clock. And she says you and Gregory can play with Bunny. Mary's looking after him."

"She's not looking after me," Morann announced. "Mary's bossier than Kath."

"But——"

"You think I'm not trustable here," Morann accused her mother.

"Oh no, dear!"

"Then prove it!" Morann challenged. "Let me just stay home."

"But——" Mom looked at her anxiously. "Morann, you . . . you wouldn't switch on the stove or——"

"I wouldn't switch on the stove or leave the

taps running or let strangers into the house or light matches or forget to change my diapers." The words ended on a shrill note, at the edge of tears.

"Well . . ." Mom obviously did not want to show that she didn't trust her. "If . . . if you're quite sure you'll be all right here alone . . . oh, dear! Perhaps I should have let you go with Sarah."

"Who wanted to go with Sarah?" Morann hid her misery in a fresh spurt of bead-hunting. But she looked up to say, "And please don't keep phoning to see if I'm all right, because I'll probably be out here in the hammock reading and I won't hear the phone. I'll probably even have my lunch out here."

Later, Morann complimented herself on that bit about the phone, though when she said it, she didn't have a thing in mind, except maybe reading in the hammock where Neil could see her if he was really stuck for someone to talk to.

By the time her mother left, Morann had donned shorts and a shirt, eaten her cereal, and moved into the garden with a jug of lemonade and a book. And it could have been the lemonade that enticed Neil over before he even started his usual garden chores.

"Hi," Morann greeted him. "What are the trees wincing about this crummy morning?"

"Your face?" he suggested, helping himself to

the lemonade. "So. They wouldn't take you."

"Huh! Who wants to go scrambling over logs and running into wasps' nests?"

"You do. So why don't you smarten up a bit? Why don't you show them you're not a goop?"

Neil left her to think that one over. Then, instead of weeding in the cool of the early morning, he went off on his bike. Probably to see Angus.

Really high and dry, Morann began thinking of what he had said. Why don't I smarten up? Why don't I show them I'm not a goop? "Hey!" An idea hit her. The cross-valley bus went by the corner about eight-thirty. And it could drop her off near the foot of Devil Mountain. Sarah had said so, in case Mom needed the car.

She rushed into the house and made a fast peanut butter sandwich. She snatched up a few cookies and poured the rest of the lemonade into an old plastic bottle with a handle. Then she jammed a sun hat on her head. She even locked the back door and cached the key. She'd show them who was a goop.

Today she was going to be one hundred percent sensible. She wouldn't let herself be panicked into stupid words or stupid actions. There would be no show-off stuff. Nothing but plain common sense, she vowed as she sprinted down to the corner. Wow! Were they going to be surprised when she just strolled up to them on Devil Mountain and joined their sandwich break. "No, thanks," she was going to say to Kath's reluctant offer of food. "I'm equipped."

Morann just made the bus. "Wayne's Corner," she told the driver. And she felt pretty smart about remembering it from when Sarah had looked it up. Today she was going to be right on.

"That'll be two bits."

"Oh dear! I guess I must have lost a couple of pennies. I've only got twenty-three cents." Then she added a suitably dramatic wail. "And I'm meeting my aunt and my sisters."

"Okay. Okay. Two cents isn't going to bust the company."

"Oh, thank you! Will you let me know when I get there?" She sat up front in the almost empty bus.

"Wayne's Corner," the driver called out about half an hour later. "But I don't see your folks."

"Oh, they're over there." She pointed a little low on the mountain so it looked as if she were pointing to a farmhouse.

"Okay. Have a good day."

"Thank you."

A short, hot, dusty walk along a country road took her to the foot of Devil Mountain, which wasn't much of a mountain by northwest standards. And the sight of Mom's parked car further cheered her. She was tempted to write in its dust: "The sasquatch was here." But no silly kid stuff today! she told herself firmly.

Then she caught her breath. "Sasquatch?" No! Not on little Devil Mountain.

The trail looked better than she had hoped. And even if it petered out, it wasn't going to be like getting lost in a forest and going round and round. As long as you kept going up, you'd come to the lake at the top. Then as long as you kept moving down, you'd make it back to the bottom, where it was all farms. Of course there were bigger mountains and alpine meadows behind Devil Mountain; but the farms were south and west, towards the sunset. Morann had heard Sarah say that when she was talking about the compass. And anyway, it wasn't much of a mountain. It wasn't big and jagged like those mountains where they said—— No! Morann told herself. This was no time to think about the sasquatch. There probably wasn't such a thing as a sasquatch anyway.

Morann stepped briskly onto the trail.

Actually, it was very pleasant just beyond the dusty edge. Wild pea vine made green and blue patterns under the alders. And on impulse, she snatched up a few trailing pieces and wound them around her sun hat. Then she instantly regretted the whim. The vines would only wilt and flop like a dead bird. Wild flowers always wilted so quickly and looked so sad . . . and . . . accusing? Morann swallowed, suddenly remembering the polygraph. The whole vine did seem to be trembling. *Plants react like people. They get alarmed when you threaten them. They get all excited when you even just think of hurting them.*

A line from Neil's *Wildlife* article jumped into her mind: *Could it be that when cell life dies, it broadcasts a signal to other living cells?* And the signals could leap across distances. Right now, her vine could be alerting every living thing on Devil Mountain. It could be warning every plant and every animal that Morann was a killer.

"I'm so sorry," she whispered, kneeling anxiously down on the trail. And for the first time in her life, she noticed how utterly lovely the vines were. Clusters of tiny, tiny, violet-blue sweet peas trembled along a fragile, airy green stem, sending out a delicate fragrance. "I'm so sorry," she repeated. And now there was genuine regret in her words.

It was a bad start. She sensed the rejection of the woods. Wild huckleberry and salmonberry bushes seemed to be holding their arms out across the trail to try to make her turn back. A jungle of leafy undergrowth crowded the trail on both sides, as though trying to stop it from taking Morann into the wilderness. And, as though obedient to the will of the wilderness, the trail practically petered out by the time she came to the lookout rock.

Here there was a fine view over the farms and the river and the mountains beyond the river. So she sat on the rock and nibbled one corner of her peanut butter sandwich. She took a few good swigs of lemonade.

"Ch-ach-a-t-ch!"

Morann was so startled she almost fell off the rock. But it was only a squirrel, a tiny, rusty-colored squirrel with black stripes down his back. "Hi, squirrel!" she said, eager for company of any kind.

Then her mouth dropped open. The squirrel had lifted his tiny paws and flipped his tail into the exact position of Gregory's picture squirrel. And he stayed still as a picture.

Morann found she was holding her breath. But that was silly. Any squirrel looked like that. And it was stupid to think—even for an instant—that this was Gregory's squirrel, escaped from the picture frame. Still, it would be nice to be with Kath and Robin and Sarah. Which way up from here? she wondered, scanning a couple of openings in the bush ahead.

"Left or right?" she wondered aloud, after looking back and forth between the two possibilities.

As if in answer, the squirrel chattered at her and then skipped along a dead stick, making for the opening to the right.

"Okay," Morann agreed. Her eyes followed him. He was uncannily like Gregory's squirrel. "Of course he's like Gregory's squirrel," she told herself in a whisper, "because Gregory's picture is a picture of a real squirrel." It was just that she wasn't used to being alone in a place as quiet as Devil Mountain. Or else she was too used to being with Gregory and his wild imagination.

Morann tackled the trail, which wasn't much of a trail. She had to watch sharply for the occasional blaze on a tree. At least, watching kept her mind off the quiet. It was a terribly quiet, lonely sort of place, as if no one ever came here. There was heavy underbrush you had to part with your hands, and fallen timbers you had to climb over or wriggle under. Morann began to wish she had worn jeans instead of shorts. And she began to listen harder and harder for Robin's booming voice. But there was nothing. Nothing but an uncanny silence.

Fallen timber lay crumbling, rotting away, with flabby fungi that seemed like big ears listening for something. You'd need big ears to hear anything, she thought. It was gruesomely quiet. Perhaps it was just that all the moss muffled sound and movement. Morann found herself trying to keep even her breathing quiet.

Every now and then the squirrel—or was it another squirrel?—scampered ahead as merrily as ever. One creature, at least, had not been alarmed by the signal from the dying vines. And every now and again he turned and watched her with that startling resemblance to Gregory's squirrel.

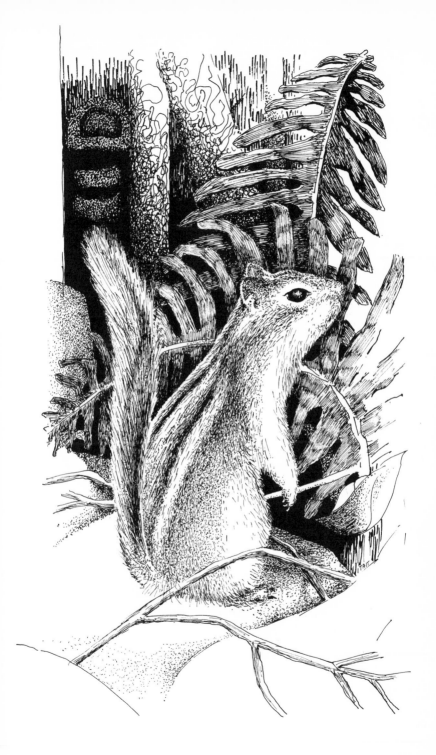

But she was not going to be silly just because she was scared. He was just a plain, ordinary, everyday squirrel who lived on Devil Mountain.

Once, watching him, she nearly barged into a Devil's Club. Devil's Club had awfully big leaves that seemed to be hiding something; it had thorns that could dig into you, people said, and really make you wish you had watched where you were going. Yet it couldn't be as poisonous as they said, she told herself. Indians used its juice for ritual purification, according to the notes that Kath kept reading out loud.

Glancing nervously about, she ran into a low branch that knocked her hat off. It startled her so that she tripped, falling headlong into a punky, decaying log. "Oooogh!" she cried out. Then, desperate to be out of the horrible forest, she picked herself up, jammed her hat back on her head, stumbled over roots, ripped her clothes on branches, and twice pitched headlong down unexpected little gulleys. The forest felt so . . . so . . . so stlalakum. Why, oh why, did Kath keep reading those awful notes? *Anything uncanny is stlalakum. The place. The thing. Stlalakums are unnatural beings in the natural world. Beings?* "Leaping leppercorns!" Now she began to glimpse dark shapes out of the corner of her eye; though when she turned to look, they were not there.

Morann was trembling when she finally emerged from the dank, dark woods into more open, parklike timber. There she realized that she was hot and very thirsty.

The sun was at its height. So she decided that giving in to hunger and thirst was better than impressing Sarah and the girls. "I've had my rations," she'd tell them; though maybe she wouldn't turn down their offer of a drink. There had been a stream. But you couldn't risk drinking from streams any more.

Morann ate the rest of her lunch. She downed the last of the lemonade and tossed her empty plastic bottle into a bush. It made a strange, hollow sound when it hit, probably hurting plants and sending out more signals ahead of her.

Thank goodness, there was the squirrel again, or some squirrel, chattering away at her. There was one friendly tribe, at least, on Devil Mountain. "Okay. Okay," she answered, eager to keep him with her. "I'm coming." If he was the same squirrel as before, he was such a lively little fellow that she wouldn't blame Gregory's squirrel for scampering away at night to join him.

Morann pulled her thoughts up short. What kind of thinking was that? At the edge of the wilderness, you needed a wild imagination the way you needed a broken leg.

"Well!" Morann took a deep, purposeful breath. She had to go on. Anyway, going on was better than going back through those dank woods, past those decaying logs with their ghastly ears.

She wished she could hear Robin's booming voice. Or Kath's brisker sounds. Surely she must be near the top now.

As she climbed on through the more open area, the heat hit her again. And she had not one drop to drink. So she glanced about for possible berries. Juice would certainly help.

She spotted some dark berries near the ground. Salal? She was sure Neil had said that plants like that were salal. And everyone knew that Indians made jam out of salal berries. Squawberry jam. She tried a tiny handful.

"Ptp! Indians can have them," she said, trying to spit out the taste. Actually, the berries tasted very, very peculiar. What if the Forestry had sprayed Devil Mountain from an airplane for bugs or blight or something? Maybe you shouldn't eat anything.

Trying to spit out every last bit of berry netted her a pinky-purple stain on her shirt. Her mouth was already pinky-purple and horribly dry.

"Phew!" It was hot. Surely she must be near the lake. Morann strained to hear her sisters. But there was only silence. Awesome silence. Not even the birds seemed to be twittering. There wasn't the usual summer hum of insects.

But she forgot the quiet as she really noticed the trees. They were like . . . like *beings*. Some branches were like drooping arms. Others were like drooping heads wrapped in a shawl.

Cedars are always droopy-looking, she told herself. Yet she knew that cedars did not usually show such a twisting of bark in their lower trunk. In fact, they were usually so straight that you could pull the thin bark off in strips. It was as if these cedars had had a dizzy childhood. "They're gruesome," Morann gasped.

Then she clapped a hand over her mouth. Even if the cedars hadn't caught her words, they could tell what she was thinking. "Actually," she said, as loud as she could, "they look kind of . . . of artistic." Morann wasn't used to coming up with compliments. And what she was used to coming up with, a loud voice, just did not seem to happen on Devil Mountain. Her voice was a whisper. And when she swallowed, her mouth was dryer than ever.

She was terribly tempted to turn and run. But behind her were all those dark, creepy woods. And she was obviously at the top now, where there was sure to be company. Anyway, after getting so close to Stlalakum Lake, she was not going to go home defeated.

The others might have found a better, quicker way up, she thought. Perhaps the opening to the left of the lookout rock was the one she should have taken. But once she got to the lake, even if the others had already come and gone, she'd be able to circle round and find their trail. Robin was sure to have left deep footprints from dropping out of trees onto imaginary sasquatches. The trail would be easy to find, and it would be easy to tear down the mountainside and catch up with them before they reached the car.

And if she didn't? She had no bus fare, even if she made the evening bus. In a proud moment she decided she'd hitchhike before she'd phone home and ask to be rescued.

Morann scooted on past the twisted, stunted cedar trees, half expecting one of the drooping arms to reach out and grab her. The trees knew she was scared, and that made being scared worse. There wasn't any use swaggering, because every stupid little scaly leaf knew what was in her mind. That is, every beautiful little scaly leaf knew what was in her mind.

"Stlalakum Lake!"

Suddenly, there it was, not much bigger than a duck pond, even if it was bottomless, according to Kath's notes.

There was no sign of anyone.

There was no sound. The silence seemed as deep as the gloomy green water.

Perhaps it was its depth that made the lake look so dark. Or perhaps it was the reflection of all the dark conifers crowding around its edges.

Morann leaped sideways to keep from stepping on three snails. There were so many snails!

"Ugh! . . . I mean . . . I'm sure snails are good for something." She really did wish she had never heard of Neil's psychogalvanic whatever-it-was. It was creepy, knowing that everything around her could hear what she was thinking; while she couldn't even hear a bee or a mosquito.

She certainly was not going to rest there. But she did have to sit down long enough to empty out her sneakers, which were full of dirt and bits of bark. She'd need good feet to tear down the mountainside.

The thought of snails kept her from flopping down on the ground. And the only other likely spot was the wide, low branch of a solitary alder tree, reaching out over the water. So she sat there, took off her right shoe, emptied it into the lake, and——

"Ch-ach-a-t-ch!"

The unexpectedness of the squirrel's chatter, in all that awful silence, startled her so badly she threw up her hands, grabbed wildly to save herself from falling in, and let go of the sneaker. It went down, down, down, down into the bottomless water.

Morann was trembling as she leaned back against a higher branch to think of what she could tie around her foot.

5

_____

ABOVE, AS MORANN LOOKED UP, THERE WAS A HIGH small cloud. It seemed to be moving straight towards her.

It was obviously caught in a downdraft, she told herself. A downdraft could move a cloud along fast and also stretch it out until it looked like a great white plume with its quill pointing towards Stlalakum Lake. Wasn't there something about cold little mountain lakes attracting clouds? Something natural?

But wasn't there also something unnatural about a sky plume in Kath's notes? She couldn't remember what the note said.

Morann took a firm grip on the branch. What she saw was simply a cloud. It was simply a cloud caught in a downdraft. And it was silly to feel peculiar about a cloud. It was just that the awful silence and the dank woods and the fungus ears and Neil's polygraph were all adding up in her imagination. That was all there was to it.

Still she did feel very, very strange watching that white plume of cloud come down. Her scalp prickled.

Its point touched down on the lake. And the feathery white cloud was fog. Only it was fog writhing in a fantastic way. Wisps of vapor were darting in and out of each other. It was as though a million tiny ghosts were milling about together.

She tightened her grip on the branch. The cold of the lake and the heat of the day were simply agitating the mists. She was getting as bad as Gregory, she decided, when all at once she knew she heard voices coming out of the fog.

The voices were misty. They had a floating quality, as if they were drifting to her slowly. One came from up high and was high-pitched. The other voice was lower. And the two seemed to be arguing in a strange, ghostly way, lifting the end of each important word up into a wail of protest.

"You're too eager," the deeper voice said. "Give her time." The word "time" was stretched out into "tiiiiiiiiiime."

"Why? She has come alone to the lake, hasn't she?"

Too scared to run, Morann clutched the branch and glanced nervously about. Perhaps someone had followed her up the mountain. Maybe it only seemed as if the voices were coming out of the cloud.

"She has come alone to the lake," the higher voice repeated. "And see her mouth. She has eaten the berries." "Berries" was a wail of triumph.

Morann clapped a hand over her mouth. The berries!

The deeper voice spoke now. "She has eaten the berries. Yes. But give her time. We used to give them four days in the wilderness in the old days."

Four days in the wilderness? For what? In what old days? Morann's heart was thumping so hard it would have wakened her if she'd been dreaming. So she *wasn't* dreaming.

The mists began to lift. And the cloud rose up as fast as it had come down. "It's caught in an updraft now," she whispered, trying to believe that that was all there was to it. As it moved away, again she could see that it was still shaped like a white plume, a sky plume. "I *am* getting as bad as Gregory," she said, speaking to hear herself speak. She leaned back to pull herself together.

"Morann!"

It was Robin's voice, booming across the little lake. "What are you doing up here?"

"Just . . . hiking," Morann answered in about the smallest voice she had ever used in talking to a sister. And she sagged with such sudden relief that she almost fell into the water.

Her relief was followed by a surge of joy. They had been the voices. Robin and Kath had put on an act, trying to scare her. Well! she certainly was not going to let them know that she had fallen for it. So she sat where she was, dangling her legs as if she hadn't a care in the world.

"Watch it!" Kath cautioned as she came closer. "You know what they say about stlalakum lakes. There are subterranean channels joining them to the open sea. And those channels can suck you in."

Morann tried to moisten her lips and speak out in her usual way. "Where were you?" she demanded. "I thought I was all alone. I didn't hear a thing." There! That would show them that they hadn't scared her. But, had they seen the strange cloud, too?

"We were exploring back there in the bush," Robin told her. "The remains of an old Indian building."

"We were hunting for artifacts," Sarah added, from a few yards behind the two girls.

"You've lost your shoe," Kath accused as Morann moved from the lone alder and hop-stepped to meet them.

"It fell in."

"And you're not going to dive for it," Kath told Robin firmly. "Maybe there really are subterranean channels sucking things out to sea. Lucky you didn't fall in with your sneaker, Morann."

"Yeah." The word showed more relief than Morann intended. In spite of the hot day, she felt a shiver. There was something weird about the place. *Anything uncanny is stlalakum.*

"Well," Kath said, her mind on the practical. "How are you going to hike down the mountain in a sock?" She opened her shoulder kit, took out foam-lined adhesive tape and small scissors, and proceeded to improvise a sandal. "You're lucky the deer made such a good trail."

"Yeah," Morann agreed. And again the word held more relief than she had intended. "No trouble about the trail." So they had found a good trail. They would. But she certainly was not going to admit that she hadn't been so smart. She had followed a squirrel, a nutty thing to do. Yet she managed a touch of swagger as they started off for home.

Nobody said a thing about a cloud.

Nobody said a thing about scaring her.

Morann was careful not to lag last in the line. And she was awfully glad to see the car, there, at the foot of Devil Mountain.

"Morann!" Mom cried when they got home. "We were nearly out of our minds. You said you'd be all right alone."

"I was all right." Now that she was safely home and could smell chili con carne, she felt as if she had been perfectly all right, even up there on the edge of Stlalakum Lake.

"And you promised."

"I promised I wouldn't switch on the stove or light matches or let strangers into the house. I didn't say anything about not moving out of the yard, did I, Mom?"

"No, but . . . but going alone up a wild mountain!"

Sarah broke in. "It's my fault. I should have taken Morann. She was more than equal to the climb. And at her age, I'd have proved it the way she did."

Morann fled. Kind words always made her eyes wet. She rushed into a bathroom and dawdled over getting cleaned up. What a day!

It was only much, much later, when she was in bed, that she let herself start to think things over. That cloud. Those voices. It couldn't have been Kath and Robin putting on an act or they'd have been crowing about scaring her. And that squirrel! Of course it might not have been one but a half dozen squirrels. She glanced at Gregory's picture. And in the dim light, it did look as if its little black eyes were twinkling at her. As if it knew something.

Most of all, though, it was the voices that haunted her.

"Sheeeeeee has eaaaaaaaaaaaten the berrieeeee- eeees."

The berries! Maybe what she had thought was salal was one of those plants that gave you hallucinations. "Leaping leppercorns!" she gasped. Hallucinations could come back, even if you never ate another berry!

Fortunately, the day's climb had tired her and she went off to sleep rather quickly.

It must have been two in the morning when the voices woke her. They were the same two misty voices she had heard at the lake. Only now they were floating into her bedroom.

"You're tooooooooooo eager," the deep voice was saying, as it had said before. And its long-drawn-out words slipped into Morann's consciousness so gently that she didn't even open her eyes.

Now the higher voice was protesting, as before. "What if they dooooooooon't let her gooooooooooo up that mountain again? What if they make her promise she won't gooooooooooo?"

Up that mountain? They wouldn't have to make her promise, Morann thought. No one could pay her to go back up that mountain. She shut her eyes very tightly. If there really was something there at the window, she did not want to see it.

"Perhaps it didn't mean a thiiiiiiing," the deeper voice pointed out.

The high voice went even higher with wailing protest. "A child? Going aloooooooone. There. And even eating the berieeeeees." Then the voice lowered slightly and seemed to fill with longing. "A child. On the old, old quest. It has been so loooooooong!"

Morann wasn't sure what a quest was. She did know it had something to do with a prince or a knight or somebody going off to find a treasure. Could there be a treasure cached up there on Devil Mountain! Was that why Indians frightened white people off with tales about two-headed snakes and big, hairy sasquatches? Those might have been Indians, pretending to be ghostly voices up there at the lake. Well, it would have to be some treasure to make her dare Devil Mountain again.

She couldn't see a thing, especially since she had grabbed the sheet and wound it round her head. She was not going to look. She was dreaming, of course; but she certainly was not going to look and make such a crazy dream any crazier than it already was.

"I dooooooon't think this child is braaaaaaave enough," the deeper voice said, still lifting the end of each important word into a ghostly wail.

"Oh, give her tiiiiime!" the higher voice pleaded.

Time? For what? Morann pulled the sheet more tightly around her head. She heaved herself over, in order to face away from the window. And she hit the floor with a thump.

"What's the matter, dear?" It was Mom's voice, coming towards her down the hallway.

Morann fought her way out of the entangling sheet to see her mother hovering near the door at the edge of a patch of moonlight.

"I guess I fell out of bed." For some reason or other she glanced up at the picture. And she had the terrifying idea that she saw the squirrel flip his tail into place.

"Well, get back in, dear," Mom said before she vanished.

Morann got back in and quickly wound the sheet around her head.

But the voices had vanished, too.

At breakfast, Kath and Robin kept chattering about Devil Mountain.

"Did we tell you we found the remains of an old Indian building?" Robin asked her mother.

"Not more than four times, dear."

"Well, if nobody would live up there, like they say, that building must have been a witchdoctor's hangout."

Sarah added a fact that was obviously confirmation. "We could make out just enough paint

and carving to decide that the decoration was the Seexqi."

"Seexqi?" Morann's query was little more than a whisper. Actually, she didn't know why she asked. She certainly was not keen to find out what the Seexqi was.

But Kath's notebook was there like a flash with the dreadful information:

"Seexqi. Double-headed snake. Comes to the surface of certain small lakes and shoots a head out each end. Body is big and black. Heads are round with round ears and red circles at the top. Makes a noise like a duck, but much much louder. 'If you saw that animal you would not dare to turn round and run away.'"

"Why not?" Morann couldn't understand why she kept asking for more, nor why her voice was so small.

"The Seexqi had terrible power. Even its image on a house or a totem pole had such power that people didn't approach it until they had eaten of a certain plant or certain berries. But you had to stand and face it. 'If you ever turned your back on that animal, you would start to spin around until you were dizzy. And you would go out of your mind. Or drop dead.'"

"Wow!" The twisted trunks of the stunted cedars flashed into Morann's mind. Maybe people had turned and run away from the awful thing they had seen in the lake, and had started to spin and spin. Maybe they had grabbed young cedar trees and hung on for dear life. Hung on and twisted the little trees until they had been held in those twists by dead hands. Maybe, if you looked carefully under those trees, you would find the bones. Everything fitted in too well! There *were* unnatural beings in this natural world. More and more she just had to believe it.

"I don't seem to be hungry this morning," she said, pushing back her chair to leave the table and the terrible conversation.

"You overdid it yesterday," Mom said.

"And that's my fault," Sarah cut in. "If we'd taken Morann on the more leisurely trip . . ."

"Leisurely?" Robin pretended to rub aching muscles.

"Oh. You want to be counted out for the big one?" Sarah asked her teasingly.

"No sireeee!"

"Good." Sarah turned from Robin to Mom. "We're planning to camp out in those alpine meadows behind Devil Mountain. They say there's a good road part of the way in from behind, so we won't have to hike too far with our camping gear. And this time, we are taking Morann with us."

"Thank you."

There really wasn't much bounce in Morann's answer, nor much gratitude for that matter. But she simply could not say that she didn't want to go. She was not going to let them know that the idea of camping out terrified her. Not now, when Sarah positively seemed to admire her. She'd go. And she'd stick to Sarah the way a rubbed balloon stuck to a wall.

6

"WHY AM I SO WISHY-WASHY?" MORANN WAILED to herself the morning they loaded the car for the campout. She didn't want to go up into those mountains. But she was going, because she couldn't bear to have the others know that she was scared to go.

"Morann has spunk," Sarah had declared several times. And that was enough to drive Morann on.

She tucked her shirt back into her jeans. It was about fifteen minutes to countdown. So, if she was going to get out of it, she had better think of something fast. Of course she could say that she felt as if she were coming down with the flu. Only she had just put on a big, cartwheeling performance in the back garden—an act that hardly suggested she was wasting away with sickness.

Maybe she could twist an ankle, bounding with joy towards the car? Only somebody would say, "I knew you were showing off too much," and that might ruin her in Sarah's eyes. She had to go. But she really would stick tight to Sarah. And she'd insist on sleeping between Robin and Kath in the tent. She'd make it seem as if she was such a good sport she didn't mind being squashed.

"What's biting you?" Neil asked when she came out of the house, ready for the slaughter.

"What's biting you?" she countered. Neil looked about as joyous as a wet cat.

"Well. You know I've been wanting to get up into those alpine meadows before they hand the place over to the miners or the loggers or somebody?"

"Sure. So why don't you come along?" she urged him. "There's room in the car. And you've got a pup tent." It would be great to have a plain, sensible person like Neil along, a person who could make queer things seem okay.

"Oh, I'm coming."

"You are? Then why the gloom?" Robin, she guessed.

"I'm going in with Angus."

"Angus? Not that——" What she wanted to

say was: that weedy, reedy, squeaky, budding Einstein who has more gadgets than a doctor's clinic. Angus's dad, who wasn't home as much as even her own geologist father, paid for more scientific equipment for his son than the lab teacher ever got his hands on for the whole school. "What do you want Angus for? A tent pole? No, I know. With that freaky hair of his, you want him for an antenna."

"Shut up. I want him for a polygraph. He thinks he can get one."

"Naturally." Angus could get anything.

"And I could use it if——"

"Yeah," Morann broke in sympathetically, "if you lug him and ten tons of equipment into the hills for some goopy experiment."

"Wrong as usual," Neil told her. Then his voice dropped to dismal depths. "If I let him lug me in . . . without grub."

"But——" Food was a big factor in Neil's life. "That's crazy. If Angus goes without food for a few days, he'll slip out of sight down some crack in a rock."

"Oh, we're not going without food. It's just going to be grubs instead of grub."

"Grubs? Ugh!" Neil was in worse trouble than she was. "What on earth gave him that idea?"

"Who knows? Maybe I did. I've been yattering away at him about plants having a system of signals. And it must have struck him that he was overlooking one aspect of science, that maybe he ought to get closer to nature. Only his idea of getting closer to nature is to go in there and eat it. We're going to fuel our personal machines with barbecued dragonflies and fricaseed grasshoppers. And it's my own fault. I started it all with that *Wildlife* article."

"Neil, you're not really going to live on bugs?"

Neil put on the high-pitched tone usually associated with Angus. "The body is merely a mechanism that needs fuel to operate. And the disciplined mind should free itself from prejudices."

"I'll slip you a few raisins," Morann promised. "And maybe a few cooking hints. Hey! You could try dunking mosquito crisps into green caterpillar dip."

"Guck!" Neil grabbed at his throat. Then he told her in a lofty squeak, "We mustn't be betrayed by our senses."

"Well, just don't camp downwind from us." The smell of frying bacon could drive a boy out of his mind while he was eating stewed ants. "How're you going? On bikes?"

"Bikes? You know what Angus is like on a bike. Well, so does his mother. So she's driving us to the start of the trail. The whole idea of nature-in-the-wild kind of threw her. But she's willing to go along with it as long as we go in when you nice, sensible girls are going, and as long as she has some insurance against her genius absent-mindedly walking off a cliff."

"And you're the insurance."

"Anything to get my hands on a polygraph."

"And you do mean anything. Ugh!"

"You don't know how ugh. His mother bought him a book on how to survive in the wilderness, and he's kind of carried away with the whole deal. I just hope we find a lot of berries."

"Berries?" Morann's eyes went wide. By now she had definitely decided that those berries had been her downfall.

"Berries if I'm lucky."

"Yeah. Berries if you're lucky."

"What *is* biting you this morning, Morann?"

Before she had to answer, a car turned into the driveway next door.

"See you round the ants' nests," Neil said, turning to go. "And don't waste any raisins on Angus. Or sympathy. Ants won't bother him. He'll just mentally convert them into minerals and proteins and acids and stuff and down them like a space pill."

"Ready, Morann?" Kath demanded from the Fenns's driveway.

"Let's hit the trail!" Morann called back, as if she couldn't wait to be up and at it. Then, with an unexpected little shiver, she whispered to a rosebush, "Just spend your time hoping I get back!"

The boys got away first.

"Let's go!" Robin urged.

"All the time in the world," Sarah said with a lazy wave at the fresh, lovely morning. "We're going to enjoy the mountain scenery."

It took a couple of hours to wind up around the mountain highway to the point where they could park the car near a gas station and hike in to the alpine meadows. Along the way they passed the boys' car, parked in front of a restaurant.

"Guess Angus's mother insisted on one last civilized fueling of his personal machine," Morann remarked. She was quite pleased with the way everyone had laughed at her account of the boys' project. And it did give her a nice way—at long last!—to air her knowledge about psychogalvanic reflexes in plants. She began to be glad she had come.

They parked the car, slung on their packs, and walked towards the sign where the trail started. And there, at the edge of the wilderness, her earlier reluctance came back. She just did not want to go on into those mountains. She wanted to turn and run.

But she couldn't. So she pretended that she had stopped to adjust her borrowed backpack. She took a deep breath and moved on.

A patch of pea vine at the edge of the woods startled her with its resemblance to that other patch on that other trail. This time, she did not snatch up any delicate leaflets and tendrils and tiny blue-bonnet flowers to wind around her hat. In fact, she made a little spurt to pass them quickly.

"Rarin' to go, eh, Morann?" Sarah said gayly.

"Yeah. But . . . but I won't go in front. I'm not much of a pathfinder."

"You did all right on Devil Mountain."

"Yeah. So . . . I won't have to lag last either." She had no intention of lagging behind the others.

Morann stepped aside to let Kath and Robin pass her. Then she moved swiftly in, in front of Sarah. It was the middle of the march for her. Her pack was heavy, but even if she died of exhaustion, she was not going to lose her place in the line.

"Now I know why I had to come," Sarah said, about a mile along the trail. She flung her arms wide to encompass the lovely stretch of meadow and alpine trees and tiny lakes they could glimpse ahead. There were patches of blue, blue as the sky; there were banks of white, gleaming like snow; there were splashes of flame-red, and yellow, and purple-blue.

"Wild flowers," Sarah murmured, pulling her hands in to lift her hair from her neck and let it float out on the light breeze.

Kath motioned for silence and pointed to the hummingbirds darting and hovering about a cluster of columbines near the trail. Their brilliance

· 65 ·

outshone the gracefully nodding blossoms.

Almost as one, the campers slipped to the ground to watch and to ease their shoulders. Almost as one they sniffed, as a breeze carried the scent of alpine wild roses to them.

"Glorious!" Sarah whispered. "You have to see and smell and feel the pre-concrete, pre-telephone pole world to really understand the Indians' legends with their reverence for the Laws of Life. What a world they lived in!"

"Yeah," Morann agreed, with all the enthusiasm she could muster. "What a world they lived in!" Stlalakums. Two-headed snakes that blew your mind. Sasquatch giants that snatched up berry pickers. She'd have turned and run, if it hadn't meant running alone.

"The quiet!" Sarah said raptly.

"Yeah. The quiet." It was the quiet that really got you in the wilderness. Though here there was the hum of the hummingbirds' wings and a happy little twitter of unseen birds.

"This must be set aside as a national park," Sarah went on. "Nobody must be allowed to spoil this."

"Oh, somebody's working on it," Kath informed her, flipping pages in her notebook. "There's going to be a hearing in . . . let's see . . . October. I wish they'd done it sooner so there'd be a proper campsite."

"Who needs a proper campsite?" Robin demanded in a voice that scattered the hummingbirds.

"Speaking of campsites," Sarah said, beginning to scramble to her feet, "let's get in there and choose ours."

"Before the boys," Robin boomed, leaping to her feet and bounding off along the trail.

Morann hurried into her pack and up onto her feet. She had to keep her place in that line. One shoe lace was flapping; but she let it flap. She'd tie her new sneakers when they all stopped for another rest.

For the first time she really noticed how big the mountains were, looming above and beyond the meadows. These were the mountains you could see out the front bedroom window, the mountains where—— No. She made herself look at flowers close to the trail. But the mountains were so overpowering that they kept making her look at them. Sasquatches could easily live there and nobody ever see them.

They chose a spot by a small lake, just over a hummock from a creek. And they pitched their tent to face the lake, leaving space for a campfire.

"Here come the boys," Morann announced. She had been watching the trail, anxious to have sensible old Neil handy. And anyway, she liked Neil.

But in the high country, Neil was as bad as Sarah.

"This is really something!" he said to Morann, while she was slipping him a handful of raisins by the creek. And he actually ate them absent-mindedly, with his attention on the brook. Splintering against the rocks, the water was hurling up sprays of rainbows, while above, tiny blue flowers and flaming Indian paint brush held themselves untouched. "I wonder if the little blue ones keep getting startled when the water comes near," Neil said. "Man! If we could just lug a polygraph up here!"

"You sure are keen on watching plants wince," Morann said, with a hint of disapproval.

"Look, nitwit! Do you realize there could be one, big, world-wide communications system that could explain a million mysteries? It was Backster's bit about plants signalling for hundreds of miles that really blew my mind. Look. Nobody's ever really figured out how birds know where they're going when they migrate. Or fish! Nobody's ever figured out how game animals seem to know the minute the hunting season opens or closes, no matter how far away they are from a gunshot. For that matter, nobody's ever figured out how the Indians' old moccasin telegraph worked. Indians could spread the word so fast and so far that it had to be more than drums. Man!" Neil flung his arms wide to express his excitement. "What do you say to a cosmic communications network that animals—and people still close to nature—can tune in on? What do you say to that?"

Morann pulled her mind away from it as much as she could. "I say . . ." She moistened her lips and swallowed. "I say that you're not only eating bugs. You're going bugs."

"If I'm not now, I soon will be," Neil agreed dismally. "Here comes Angus with the bug catchers."

"Oh, hi, Angus." Morann greeted him, pushing the rest of the raisins well down into her shirt pocket. "Turned over any tasty logs lately?" She tried to keep her gaze off his freaky hair. "How do you find your personal mechanism chugs along on barbecued beetles?"

"Still have to find out. And the fuel supply's dead low. But we'll fix that." He pushed a butterfly net into Neil's reluctant hand. "We'll stay out for the evening flight," he informed Morann.

"See you," Neil said, going off with a wave and a grimace.

Morann fled over the hummock to the campsite. She was not going to get caught alone for one moment. Not up in the mountains. Not so close to so much that couldn't be explained.

For supper, the girls decided to just finish off their sandwiches. They lit a campfire more for ritual than for hot cocoa. And as they lazily nibbled and sipped and talked, they watched the flames and the upward flight of the odd spark. And the evening shadows stretched out on the forested slopes of the mountains. They crept in, over the lake and the meadows toward the lone little campfire.

"Just smell the wood smoke," Sarah suggested softly.

When they had finished eating, they didn't just sit around singing cheerful things like "Found a Peanut." Sarah was bent on a meaningful visit to the wilderness. That meant looking and listening.

"It's so utterly glorious," Sarah said reverently. "The air is like ginger ale."

"Chilled ginger ale," Kath agreed, pulling on a sweater.

"And the mountains!" Sarah went on raptly. She made an airy wave towards the rosy glow lingering on one high ridge. "The birds." She indicated a nighthawk, swooping like a swallow to catch an insect on the wing above the lake's edge. "And just listen!"

Morann tried not to. In fact, when she was sure nobody was looking, she plugged her ears with two wisps of cotton she had managed to sneak from Kath's first-aid kit.

But she could still hear Sarah.

"Here I can believe," Sarah was saying in hushed tones. "Here I can believe in the little stlalakum sprites who get into you, giving you notions of mischief."

Kath quietly opened her notebook. She laid a finger on her lips as she handed it to Morann, with a pencil flashlight. She indicated the lower left page.

Stlalakum sprites. Get into you the way light gets into water. The way an electric current gets into a motor. They make you do things you hadn't thought of doing.

Morann slipped it back to Kath as if it were a potato hot out of the glowing coals of the camp-fire. But she didn't get rid of the words so easily.

They still haunted her, hours later, huddled into her sleeping bag between Kath and Robin. She fell asleep with them running through her mind: *Stlalakum sprites. Get into you the way light gets into water. The way an electric current gets into a motor. They make you do things you hadn't thought of doing.*

There was no sound in the tent except light breathing when her eyes shot open in the middle of the night.

Not those voices again!

Morann held herself as stiff as an Indian paint brush. She realized that she must have lost her cotton ear plugs. For she could hear too well.

There was the higher voice. "Seeeeeeee!" Long-drawn-out and triumphant in its wailing way. "She has come again into the hills. I knew it. Oh, I knew it. This child is launched on the oooooooold, oooooooold quest. Oh, it has been so loooooong!"

"It's been toooooooooo long," the deeper voice protested. "She won't know how to doooooooooo it."

"We'll help her. We'll help her. The Invisibles will help her."

The Invisibles?

Morann squashed her eyes shut. She grabbed hold of Kath's sleeping bag with one hand and Robin's with the other.

If I go, they go with me!

7

NOTHING HAPPENED.

At least, as far as Morann knew, nothing happened. She was weak with relief when she opened her eyes and found that is was morning. A perfectly normal, gorgeously sunny morning in the alpine meadows. Birds were twittering. The campfire was crackling. And bacon was sizzling. She could smell it through the wide-open tent flap.

She pulled on her shirt and jeans. Then she splashed a little lake water on her face. "Brrrrr!" The water was icy. Morann darted back into the tent to get a sweater.

She ate her bacon and flapjacks with unusual relish. Somehow, things tasted wonderful up in the mountains.

"Isn't this glorious?" Sarah asked everyone in general.

"It sure is," Morann agreed. It was glorious to know that the night was safely over, glorious to realize that the terrifying visitation had been only a nightmare. Now the world was right and real again. But she was going to stick tight to Sarah just the same.

"Funny the boys aren't up yet," Kath remarked, glancing over at the two pup tents before she started putting the breakfast things back where they belonged.

"Would you be in a rush to start a day of eating bugs?" Robin countered. Always fascinated by food, she was watching Sarah tuck cheese sandwiches into small cellophane bags.

The girls were going to hike up to a ridge from which there should be a superb view of the snow-capped mountains beyond. They planned to eat their lunch there, then meander slowly back, trying to identify birds and flowers. Sarah predicted they'd be back in camp by five-thirty.

They were shouldering their daypacks when the boys emerged, arguing.

"Probably can't agree on the breakfast menu," Kath guessed. "Earth worms or lake worms."

"You lazy loafers!" Robin bellowed at them.

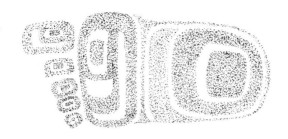

"Just for that we *will* tell you," Neil announced, heading their way. "Anyway, I guess we ought to."

"Tell us what?"

It was Angus's reedy voice that answered. "Tell you that we saw the footprints of a *gigantopithecus* while we were out hunting last night."

"Sasquatch tracks," Neil translated. And his eyes were bright with excitement.

Morann caught her breath. Sasquatch tracks! Real marks on the earth!

"Thataway," Neil went on eagerly, jerking a thumb towards a rise of land across the valley from where the girls were going. "At a spot where there's a good view of your yellow tent."

Morann caught her breath, again. *At a spot where there's a good view of your yellow tent.* He was probably watching, right now.

Angus pulled out a little black notebook. "*Gigantopithecus,*" he confirmed. "*Sixteen inch humanoid footprints.*"

Kath whipped out her slightly larger red note-book. She flipped through to a certain page and jotted down: *gigantopithecus* and *16" humanoid footprints*. Then she contributed a few more stimulating facts about the monster who had had a good view of their yellow tent: *"Body thinly covered with short hairs. Arms long like ape's. Nose flat and broad. Ears like human's. Eyes small and black like bear's. They can see in the dark. Their eyes glow like cats' eyes. Strong stench. Vegetarians.*

"I'm sure glad they're vegetarians," Robin butted in.

Kath made a patient face, then continued reading from her notebook *"Indian quote. 'They're not animals, they're people!' "*

"I'm still glad they're vegetarians."

"Being vegetarians explains why they only grab Indian girls out picking berries," Neil observed. "Skilled labor on the food front."

"Berries." Morann scarcely breathed the word. Somehow, sooner or later, berries always got into it.

Kath glanced about for attention. She had one more fact about the sasquatches. And she gave it to her fellow campers as if she were handing them a shield and buckler. "They're timid."

Neil motioned Morann aside.

"The way I figure it," he excitedly mumbled to her, "is that the signals went out. The sasquatches picked them up. And one of them came around to check on us."

"But——" Neil made sasquatches seem as likely as squirrels, as actual as grizzly bears. He made his silent communications network seem as real as the radio. "But——"

"But nothing!" he warned her. "You stay right with the others, eh?"

"Don't worry! I might even tie myself to Sarah."

"Nyah! You're safe enough. They know white people are bad news. They'll keep their distance. You know they always hit for the timber." He flicked his towel at her before going on over the hummock to the creek.

"Angus is really quite intelligent," Kath remarked, following the boys with her eyes. "*Gigantopithecus.* That's a good word."

Morann preferred the word "timid."

"Good bug hunting!" Robin called after the boys.

They merely acknowledged her malicious wishes with a wave of their towels as they disappeared around a small stand of dark alpine firs.

"Coming, Morann?" Kath demanded.

"Oh . . . uh . . ." Morann did not intend to say what she did. She didn't even think of saying it. The words seemed to say themselves. "I promised I'd help Neil out." She felt her own eyebrows rising in amazement. She *had* promised to help him out with food; but what was happening now had nothing to do with raisins.

"Hey, yeah!" Robin boomed. "That poor guy does need a little help from his friends."

"His friends," Morann heard herself say. "He's got enough trouble without you dropping down on him or trying to wrestle him, or maybe even trying to gag him with a worm." Now, why am I getting rid of Robin? she thought with alarm. When I planned to stick tight to anybody and everybody. What's got into me?

Then she gasped. *Stlalakum sprites. Get into you the way light gets into water. The way an electric current gets into a motor. Make you do things you hadn't thought of doing.*

Maybe stlalakum sprites were the voices' *Invisibles.* The Invisibles who were going to help her on the quest. But she couldn't seem to cancel her own announced decision to go with the boys. Instead, she found herself repeating it. "I promised I'd help Neil out."

"Okay," Sarah agreed, eliminating her last hope. "You'll be all right with Neil."

I won't! I won't! Morann wanted to scream it. Yet she seemed to have been struck dumb. And it was terrifying.

She also seemed to have been struck motionless. She simply could not move an inch until her aunt and her sisters had disappeared behind a clump of squat, dark evergreens. Then, to her greater alarm, she found herself darting out of sight, behind the tent, quick, before the boys came back. When she just desperately wanted to stay with people, she found herself scurrying off, farther and farther away from the boys and the girls.

It couldn't really happen. Not really. Not in broad daylight.

Only it was happening. And it seemed to have been planned.

The girls thought she was with the boys. The boys thought she was with the girls. Nobody was going to look for her until after five-thirty. She was walking farther and farther away from the campsite. And she could not seem to stop.

"Leaping leppercorns!" she gasped, when the full force of it hit her.

"Do not conjure up those grasping immortals!" a weird little voice thundered at her.

Morann stopped dead in her tracks. And her scalp prickled. The voice was like a great, commanding voice that had been compressed into a small voice. There was power there, vibrant in every word.

A shimmer of pearl flashed up onto a hummock of grass. It was a little person. Yet it wasn't a little person.

A UFO has landed, Morann thought. A flying saucer. It's a little being from Outer Space.

It was a little person. Yet it wasn't a little person. It was as if floating robes and veils had drifted down onto a bundle of energy shaped like a miniature human. The stuff of the robes and veils was gossamer, showing *nothing* underneath them; it was like spun mother-of-pearl, like the lining of a seashell. Only, instead of having the pale, iridescent greens and blues and pinks running hodgepodge into each other, these pearly tints shifted and shimmered into the squared oval eye-shapes you always saw on Northwest Coast Indian decoration. They seemed to vibrate like aspen leaves set dancing by a lively breeze. Morann felt that the little figure could lift off like a twister-wind if it wanted to, or streak off like a comet.

"You are welcome to the Wild." Again the voice startled her with its compressed power. "But do not conjure up those grasping immortals! They are unwelcome aliens in the Wild."

Aliens? Then this little being *must* belong. "But—— I didn't conjure up anybody," Morann said in humble self-defense. She seemed to be herself again. Scared stiff.

"I distinctly heard you summoning leprechauns, though your pronunciation leaves something to be desired."

Leprechauns? The conversation was getting weirder and weirder. But it did seem to be of this Earth and not of Outer Space. *You are welcome to the Wild.* The shimmering little being belonged

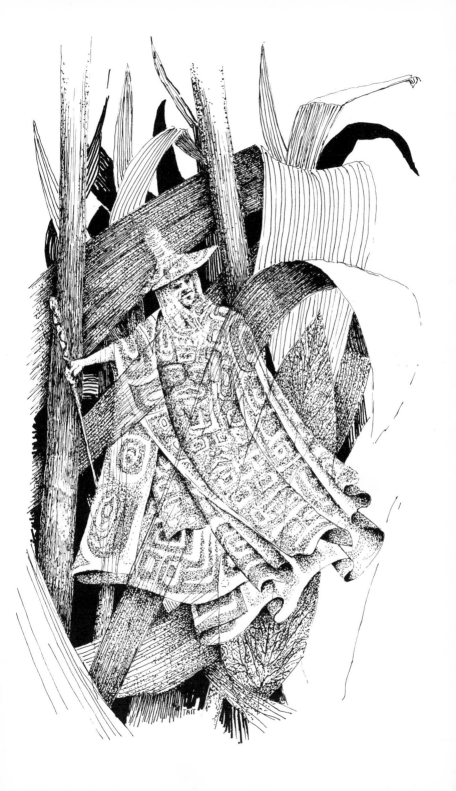

in the wilderness. Morann gasped. *Stlalakums.* Of course. This was some sort of stlalakum. It belonged here and resented aliens. But why would it resent leprechauns?

"Avaricious little men with one thing on their mind, a pot of gold," the mighty mite of a voice answered her unspoken question. "Always putting it into people's heads to root around for gold."

Could it be that the ancient quest was for gold, cached in the ground? And this little guardian of the gold was angry that the voices were going to let someone find it? Morann felt a tiny thrill of anticipation bubbling up through her terror.

The immense little voice thundered on. "Inviting destruction. Like the sea serpent."

"Sea serpent?" Of course, Indian legends said there were sea serpents. And white people did keep claiming that they had sighted one just off the coast, near Victoria mostly. But only now did Morann really believe them.

Neil's idea flashed into her mind. "What do you say to a cosmic communications network that animals—and people still close to nature—can tune in on?"

Perhaps there was all sorts of information about the world that white people were too brash and busy to pick up. Indians, who had lived close to nature might be much more knowledgeable about the natural world. They had always claimed that plants responded to what people did and said and thought. And now scientists like Cleve Backster were finding out that it was true. Well, Indians had also claimed that there were unnatural beings like sea serpents and lake snakes and stlalakum sprites. So why shouldn't that be true, too?

Morann blinked hard, twice. But the shimmering little whatever-it-was was still right there on the hummock of grass in front of her. And how could you not believe in what *was?*

The small being was still angry about the unnatural creatures who did not belong in the stlalakums' land. "No sea serpent was seen on this coast before the white men came." The tone lumped sea serpents and white men together as undesirable immigrants. "I've no doubt a sea serpent slithered along in front of those old sailing ships, luring the greedy fur traders and the greedy whalers and the greedy gold seekers to our great Stlalakum Wild."

"But——"

"I am not But," the little whatever-it-was informed her. "Please address me as Siem."

"Si-EM." Morann repeated the name carefully. And possibly because she was so scared, it came out bluntly in that loud voice of hers.

"No. SiEM." The small being poured a world of respect into the name. "It means Respected One. Noble Person."

"SiEM." Morann bowed a little as she said the word.

"That's better. Now, follow me!"

The order was unnecessary, for Morann could not help following the pearly shimmer on and on and on to a very tiny lake behind a dark stretch of trees. There they stopped, at the edge of a forested slope.

"Now. Sit down! And get on with the quest!"

"Sit down? . . . and get on?" The orders seemed a little at odds with each other.

"Yes. You don't imagine we are going to cart that big, hulking body of yours around, do you?"

"I . . . hope not." And that was the truth.

"Part of you will do."

"*Part* of me?"

"You do know that you have five parts?" The vibrant voice was a trifle impatient.

"Five?" Arms, legs, head, body, and . . . and mind, maybe? "But——" She really could not spare any of her parts.

"Yes. Five parts: body, soul, shadow, vitality, and special gift—if you're worthy of a special gift yet." Siem obviously doubted it. "All we'll move is your vitality."

"Vitality?" Morann realized that her part of the conversation was not exactly scintillating. But then, she was used to saying things that sounded stupid, even when she wasn't caught up in this weird world Siem called the Wild.

"Do not quibble over the word!" Siem commanded. "It is not my fault that your tribe has no really adequate translation for *smistiux*. Call it vitality if you wish. Call it thinking. Whatever you call it, it cannot weigh much in your case. I may as well be frank with you. I think your voices have sadly misjudged your potential. Still, they say you are ready for the quest, and I am desperate enough to humor them. So sit down! And get on with it!"

Morann sat down against a wiry clump of heather.

"I've got to be dreaming."

"All right. Call it dreaming. Perhaps dreaming is an acceptable translation."

Morann shook her head to clear it. She blinked her eyes hard. But it didn't change a thing. Siem was still there, shimmering against the green.

"Lean back! Look up!"

There it was again, a cloud moving down towards the tiny mountain lake! And as it moved down, it stretched out into a white plume.

Morann sat stunned. Spellbound, she watched the cloud.

She could not have moved away from the clump of heather if she tried.

When it finally touched down, she could see that it was full of thousands of tiny beings like Siem, but with mists instead of pearly robes to mark their vibrant, darting, swirling shapes.

"Do not be alarmed. It is just a very lively Band of Invisibles."

"Just a . . ." Morann swallowed.

This was going to be a bad trip.

8

NOBODY COULD POSSIBLY GO TO SLEEP SO EARLY IN the morning, Morann reasoned. Nobody could doze off when the mountain air was so wonderfully fresh and invigorating. So she could not be dreaming.

Yet, how could she not be dreaming? How could what seemed to be happening really be happening?

There was her own self down there, leaning against the heather in the familiar bluejeans, checkered pink shirt, mauve sunhat and green daypack. And here was *she*, looking down at herself through moving wisps of vapor. Here was she, being swirled up into the bright morning air by the Band of Invisibles Siem had summoned, the Band of Invisibles that had arrived as a sky plume.

Part of you will do. So part of her was lifting off from the earth, leaving the rest of her sitting there like a turned-off radio. Part of her was detached from the rest of her.

"But——"

It couldn't really be happening!

Yet, if it *was* happening, then it could be, couldn't it? And she certainly could see her own forlorn figure below, looking more and more lone and lost in all that sweep of mountain and meadow and little blue lakes. From higher and higher, she looked smaller and smaller, more and more alone, more and more vulnerable.

What if a bear came along? Or a big, hairy sasquatch? A sasquatch *had* looked at the campsite. He might be looking—right now!—at that helpless girl. He could easily swoop her up and carry her off into the wilderness that loomed over every meadow.

"I wouldn't worry about the sasquatch," she heard Siem saying. "He is the pitiful buffoon of our great Stlalakum Wild. Big as a grizzly, yet timid as a rabbit." The compressed power of the voice was touched with both scorn and pity. "It's too long a story to tell you at the moment; but perhaps I can make you understand." In a slow, patient, simple-words-for-simple-people way, Siem explained the sasquatch:

"No longer quite an animal, not yet quite a human, the sasquatch is caught in a terrible two-way pull, which the Indians understand." The voice seemed to caress "Indians." "They understand that every time a white hunter takes a shot at him, mistaking him for a brown bear, the poor creature decides that it would be better to be a human. So he strides out and snatches up an Indian girl who might be able to help him take on human ways. But after trying to cope with the way a human thinks, he always lets her escape. He always goes thankfully back to being just a sasquatch—until the next time a hunter nearly kills him."

"Well, what if . . . if one's like that now? Deciding he wants to be human, I mean. And what if he comes along down there and . . . ?"

"A sasquatch may be more than a little confused, Morann. But he is smart enough to know that that girl down there lacks her wits at the moment. She could not teach anyone anything. So she is safe from a sasquatch."

"I sure hope so!" And from a bear? She stopped herself from asking that one. For she really did not want to know what might happen if a bear came along.

Yet, again, Siem picked up her thinking and was clearly annoyed by it. "You are all the same.

Distrustful. It must be from the tales you hear. Tales that make the Wild a dreadful place full of dripping red claws and bared fangs. Tales that turn even our friendly wolves into fearsome, blood-thirsty villains. 'The Big Bad Wolf!' they tell you. 'The Wicked Dragon! The Sly Fox! The Satanic Serpent!' "

"But——"

"I am not But, Morann. As I told you before."

"I'm sorry, Siem," Morann whispered. And that was the truth. She didn't want to create any problems when she was not only away up in the air without visible means of support, but also away down in the mountains without visible means of protection.

As if rushing away from further questions, Siem darted off, scattering tiny, vapor-robed Invisibles out of the way, out of the path of the imperious Respected Person.

One of the scattered Invisibles must have bumped right into Morann. For suddenly she was caught up in a moment of soaring and swooping and lifting, of riding the air currents. Was this how a bird felt? she wondered. Glorious with freedom!

Only they weren't really free. They were going somewhere. The swirling, mist clad Band of Invisibles was under strict control. And her smistiux was close enough to the edge of the foggy sky plume to see occasionally the features of the land they were moving over: glorious mountains, then mountains giving way to the mighty ocean. She glimpsed its sparkle ahead, where the sea began in a clean, green fringe of islands.

Except for brief glimpses, her view of the wilderness coast was filmed over by vaporous wisps of the Invisibles' veiling. And this gave it a visionary vagueness.

As they neared the ocean, Siem shimmered towards her, down the long path through the sky plume. The Noble One gestured below. "The Stlalakum Wild!" Now the vibrant voice seemed full of worship. But, as always when Siem picked up Morann's thinking, it gained a threat of thunder. "Worship is worthship, in case you've forgotten."

"I . . . haven't . . . forgotten, exactly," Morann answered in self-defense. How could you forget what you'd never even heard? *Worship was worthship?*

Again Siem gestured downward. But now the agitated shiftings and shimmerings of the pearly robes suggested a compressed Fury. "As I suspected, there he is."

Morann scanned the islands below, and the sparkling channels between them. Then a darkness in the water made her gasp. "It's a . . . a sea serpent!" What else could it be? A dark form was undulating through the waters. So it was true. There really was a sea serpent, as so many people had claimed there was.

"Certainly there is a sea serpent," Siem told her. "And remember, Morann! Both his heads have poison fangs."

"*Both* his heads? Leaping lep—I mean, Gollllly!" There *were* two heads, one at each end of the dark, slithering body. But why did *she* have to remember? Was the sea serpent a dragon guarding the gold that lay at the end of the quest? Or waiting for it? Was he going to slither up the subterranean channel to some lake in the mountains as soon as she had found it? And come at her with his two sets of poisoned fangs!

"Yes. Two heads. Two mouths. The greedy monster! Even you can see that he does not belong here."

"But——"

Morann stopped herself from pointing out that the Seexqi had two heads, yet it seemed to belong here.

"The Seexqi has two heads so that it can look itself in the face," Siem retorted, just as though Morann had spoken. "But the sea serpent's heads have nothing to do with facing the Truth. He has no feelings for the ways of the Wild. He does not belong here. Like the rest of the creatures who do not belong here, he came only to get. The Blind Beast!"

"Get?" Morann asked it humbly. She knew that Siem was furious because she, Morann, did not seem worthy of a quest. Was the Noble One angry because Morann hoped there might be gold at the end? The quest wasn't her idea. And if that sea serpent was part of the deal, it wasn't her quest, even if a whole mountain of gold was waiting.

Obedient to a gesture from Siem, the Band of Invisibles dropped lower.

But it wasn't the speed of descent that made Morann gasp. "Don't drop me off here!" she screeched, alarmed by the sudden movement.

Another flashing gesture must have sent a stlalakum sprite into Morann again, for she found herself happy, secure instead of scared stiff.

We must look like a fluffy, white, plume-shaped cloud, she was thinking as they drifted lower, past a crescent of pale sand.

The shaft of the foggy feather finally touched down at the edge of the water. The world was green and blue and white, the colors clean and strong and lovely.

"The Stlalakum Wild," she said softly, with a hush of reverence that almost matched Siem's. The splashing of the water and the crying of the sea birds were music to Morann.

Then, as suddenly as before, her serenity left her.

"Look what he has done this time!" Siem thundered.

Morann couldn't see what the sea serpent had

done. But as the sky plume drifted slowly along, trailing misty veils over grey rocks, she could see what some other unwelcome alien had done. Ugly black blobs scarred the ocean-washed rocks where tidal pools caught the sun's shine. And sea birds lay dead in their oil-ruined feathers. But the sea serpent had not done that. Offshore drilling had done that, or a storm-wrecked oil tanker.

"There is his sign," Siem countered in a voice that permitted no argument, spoken or unspoken. "Those renegade Invisibles of his always leave his sign, Morann."

Now the sky plume hovered over his sign, a tangle of kelp drifted or blown into the great S of a two-headed serpent. And, as though to indicate that this was the signature of a sea serpent, several ribbons of seaweed had been dribbled along it like the wave patterns Gregory made with blue crayons when he was drawing his sailboats with ducks' feet underneath them.

"Those renegade Invisibles of his may be braggarts, Morann. But they never claim to have done what they have not done."

But how? Morann stopped to think. Maybe the sea serpent had rammed the tanker or the oil rig. Yet why would he do that? Wouldn't oil spoil the sea for him also? Siem must mean something else he had done, something she hadn't noticed.

Suddenly there was something she did notice. They were drifting close to the awful sea serpent.

They were moving so low that the bottom veils were trailing on the water beside the monster. And she was being swirled and swooped lower and lower along the edge of the sky plume.

"Do I have to get near him?" she gasped in sheer panic.

"Not if you are not serious about the quest."

"Oh, I'm not. I'm not, Siem."

"I thought not. Well. Your voices can not say that I did not try, can they?" Siem's voice and the sky plume lifted like an elevator.

But Morann's spirits fell. The quest was called off. What if I've blown my only chance to be wealthy? she thought grimly. What if the end of the quest really was a treasure? What if it was meant to be hers, and she was only being tested for bravery? Would she, all her life, despise herself as a coward? Maybe. But, more likely, all her life, she'd be baffled and haunted by the Stlalakum Mystery. All her life she'd feel a failure.

Her mind went over and over what had happened. *Those renegade Invisibles of his may be braggarts, Morann. But they never claim to have done what they have not done.* Siem had said that. How much could Invisibles do? If the good ones could get into her, Morann, and make her leave her family and walk off alone into a dangerous wilderness, then why couldn't the bad ones get into a man who was steering a tanker, or into a man who was drilling for oil offshore? Was that

what had happened?

But *why* would they do it? Her mind couldn't cope with it all. It seemed fuzzy and slow. Yet she knew she wasn't dreaming. The solid land and the fluid sea were right there below her. She was gazing down at them. There was no doubt about that.

The sky plume was moving away from the ocean, faster and faster, as though caught in a jet stream. It was drifting swiftly back over the rugged coastal mountains, riding high over snow peaks and forests, on and on towards the dry belt.

In the drier interior country, the sky plume slowed and drifted downward, dipping low now and then as if Siem were checking on things.

They drifted very low over a green, fragrant pinewood, trailing their misty veils slowly enough for Morann to glimpse the wild flowers growing in a parklike wilderness. The forest floor was sun-dappled, and beautifully splashed with the flame-red of Indian paint brush, with the orange of small, delicately curled tiger lilies; it was spattered with heavenly blue lupine and with lovely wild roses.

They drifted on, slowly. Then, suddenly, they lifted a little. And Morann saw a bulldozer working, knocking down the slim, lodgepole pine trees. She caught the glint of a metal tape. "A mining crew." With a geologist father, she knew about mining exploration. She also knew that in British Columbia there could be gold anywhere, everywhere. A tingle of excitement stirred her, then a twinge of regret. Perhaps she had been a little hasty in abandoning the stlalakum quest. When she thought of it, Siem had been terribly eager to have her abandon it.

Why?

She caught a shimmering gesture. And the sky plume whisked her up and away. Obviously Siem had picked up her thinking. Was it possible that the Noble One did not want Morann to think about gold?

They were moving swiftly again, back across the pinewoods and over the mountains. Back towards the alpine meadows.

And then once again they began dropping lower. Suddenly Morann could see herself, still leaning against the heather. She looked so insignificant there among all those mountains and meadows and blue lakes. As if she really didn't matter.

One moment she was drifting down.

The next she was looking up at the sky plume, dreamily watching it lift upward into the blue sky. Then she was looking about her, blinking.

"Must be late afternoon," she mumbled, vaguely noticing where the sun was. Strangely, like a slow-motion sequence, she slipped her daypack off her shoulders. The world was not quite in focus.

Where was she? What had happened? No. She didn't really want to know.

Suddenly she was herself again, scared stiff. Where was she? How could she find her way back to the campsite? What if a bear came along? What if a sasquatch came along? Morann leaped up, snatched up her daypack, and surveyed her surroundings. Which way? Why hadn't she looked for the yellow tent when she was coming down? Why had she looked just at herself leaning there against the heather? Which way?

She glanced up the nearby slope. The tent certainly was not up that way. But if she climbed, perhaps she could get a view of the meadows and spot the tents. But she might also run into a sasquatch.

She spurted off the other way, into the meadows, towards a small stand of dark firs. Had she rounded a clump of trees, just before she reached the lake? Morann strained to remember.

When she rounded the trees, there was nothing. Nothing except more trees and more stretches of meadow, more drifts of wild flowers. There was another lake, but not the right lake.

She found that she was trembling. She had to go some way. So she rushed and stumbled towards another small stand of conifers. There, she saw another lake, but not the right lake.

A coyote howled that terrible, high, long-drawn-out howl of the wilderness. And another coyote answered.

Morann burst into tears.

"Come, come-come!" It was Siem, shimmering there before her. "We are not going to punish you for not being worthy. One of my Invisibles will get you safely back to your family."

"Oh, Siem! Thank you!" But she was thanking the thin air. Siem had vanished.

Suddenly, with a strange surge of confidence, she knew which way to go. Under control, she walked past a drift of airy, blue larkspur; the depth of the blue and the light green leaves filled her with delight. She rounded a group of trees standing dark against the sunny meadow. Skirting a bank of columbine, she stopped, enchanted by the bright hummingbirds who were darting and hovering and thrumming among the blossoms. In tune with the carnival spirit of summertime in the alpine meadows, she turned a cartwheel. Singing, she topped a rise. And there was the little lake, blue and spangled with diamonds. There was the yellow tent, bright as a buttercup.

But the sight did not make her feel like another cartwheel. Instead, she was like a pricked balloon. She sank dolefully down in a patch of rosy heather. A bad thought hit her. How was she going to explain the day's adventures?

After that runaway trip up Devil Mountain, who was going to believe that she hadn't just willfully gone off again?

If she told them the truth, who was going to believe it? Who was going to believe about the stlalakum sprites? Siem? The sky plume? The huge sea serpent?

Could she just not tell them? It was all over anyway, and maybe it could stay just a bad dream. If she left it untold, perhaps she could even begin to believe that it had been just a bad dream.

At least, if the others thought she had run away, they wouldn't know she'd been scared stiff. Sarah wouldn't know that Morann was a snivelling coward.

Her hand touched her daypack. "My lunch!" If she turned up with her lunch uneaten, the others would ask questions; and Kath was awfully sharp with questions.

She opened up the pack without much enthusiasm, and began to nibble.

The way things always turned out!

Her scowl deepened as she nibbled a little faster.

None of it was her fault! She hadn't asked to be kidnapped. But she was going to look stupid, as usual, no matter how she acted.

She was munching her apple when she caught sight of Robin's red shirt. And her shoulders dropped down. She would have to face them.

"Hey!" *If* she could catch the boys and go in with them, maybe things would work out. She knew Neil would cover for her. Oh, he'd say things; but he'd cover for her. Eagerly she scanned the meadows.

"Drat!" There were the boys, coming over a rise beyond the campsite. The way things always turned out for her! It was really infuriating.

Well, she thought, hurling her apple core at a tree, here goes any liking Sarah might have had for me.

She scrambled to her feet and slung on her day-pack. Then, walking reluctantly, like a calf being dragged towards its branding, she started off towards the campsite.

As she neared the tents, though, she managed a touch of a swagger. What else could you do when things had turned out so badly? When people were going to think you were even stupider than they already thought you were! She blinked the tears back, hard.

9

LONG BEFORE SHE WAS WITHIN EARSHOT, MORANN KNEW what they were saying:
"Where's Morann?"
"Isn't she with you?"
"Why would she be? Wasn't she with you?"
"That goopy kid!"
"Showing off again."
She delayed her arrival by routing herself around several concealing stands of dark conifers. Even so, as she reluctantly rounded the last one and swaggered up to the campsite, she was not sure of what she was going to say. She'd think of something. Probably something stupid.

Naturally it was Kath who saw her first and alerted the others. Then everyone pounced on her:

"Morann!"

"Where were you?"

"You told us you were going with Neil."

"Don't you know you can get lost in the mountains?"

"Were you trying for a helicopter rescue, with headlines?"

"What got into you?"

That question of Sarah's did it. She'd tell them the truth. "A stlalakum."

"Look!" Kath snapped at her. "This is no time to be smart aleck."

"I'm not being smart aleck." But she knew she was being loud. "I'm just telling you what got into me. A stlalakum got into me. *The way light gets into water.*" It had been that way, hadn't it? *"The way an electric current gets into a motor.* That's the truth. Take it or leave it."

"I'll leave it, thanks," Kath answered. "Look, Morann! We were out of our mind for a minute."

"Big deal! I was out of my body."

"This isn't funny."

"You're telling me it isn't funny? I was the one who was out of my body."

"Wow!" Robin boomed out cheerfully. "We really do need that lie detector, Neil."

"You sure do," Morann agreed shrilly. "Otherwise you'll never believe me, and something terrible will happen to me."

She burst into tears.

Neil and Angus fled.

"Now dear," Sarah said in a soothing tone you might use with a hysterical three-year-old, "there's no real harm done. You're back safe and sound, though I don't promise I won't handcuff you tomorrow."

"Handcuff me!" It was meant as a desperate plea. But of course it came out like brash defiance.

"And tether you right now," Robin suggested as she picked up a climbing rope and swung it like a lasso.

"I wish you would." And that was the truth. "Do you think I want to go roaming round by myself where there might be sasquatches or something?"

Sarah took a deep, patient breath. "If you didn't want to roam around by yourself, dear, why did you roam around by yourself?"

"I told you. Stlalakums." She knew it was almost a screech. But what could you do when no one believed you? "I went off alone, but I'm not dumb enough to——"

"Who says you're not dumb enough?" Robin said, defending Morann's status as the stupid member of the family.

"Stop it, Robin!" Kath ordered. Then she took up the case. "Look, Morann. Just because Sarah said you were spunky, going alone up Devil Mountain, you didn't have to let it go to your head."

"It didn't go to my head. Sarah just asked me what got into me. And I just told her what got into me. Stlalakums."

"Yeah." Kath's voice was scathing. "A stlalakum got into you and made you run away."

Sarah broke in gently. "Just tell us the truth, dear."

Morann wheeled round on her aunt. "So! You're just a phoney, going round asking wrinkled old Indians about things. You don't believe a word they say."

"Oh, we do. But——"

"But okay!" Morann challenged Sarah. "Believe it! One of them told you there are stlalakum sprites that get into people and make them do things they hadn't thought of doing. So *believe!* There are stlalakum sprites that get into people and make them do things they hadn't thought of doing. One got into me."

"All right, dear, but——"

"But don't forget we know you," Kath cut in. "Always doing something to get attention. Well, aren't you?" she demanded.

"Maybe I used to. Before things started happening."

"What things?"

"What's the use of telling you what things?

You wouldn't believe me. The only person who'd believe me is Gregory."

"*I'd* believe a mousie got into your shoe," Robin assured her. Then she appeared to reconsider that statement. "I would?"

"Ooooooo!" Morann could have spat fire.

"Girls!" Sarah cautioned them. "I declare a moratorium on stlalakums until we've eaten."

"Me too." Robin scurried about, finding dry twigs.

Kath darted for the frying pan.

"I'm not hungry." Morann didn't mean it to sound so blunt. But it was infuriating, the way things always turned out for her.

"I'll eat your share," Robin offered.

"Go ahead, greedy guts!"

"Girls! . . . Robin, get some water, eh?" Sarah took over the firelighting while Kath dug out flour to make bannock.

Morann just flopped down, fuming. It was better to feel mad than scared. Yet she did so wish there was some way to tell them what had happened to her, and have them understand and crowd protectingly around her. She began to sob softly.

"Oh, come on, Morann!" Sarah urged briskly. "We're up in the magnificent mountains. And we're going to have a magnificent bannock. Kath's special."

"With magnificent hydrated dehydrated scrambled eggs," Robin added, slopping down a collapsible plastic pail of water. Then she began to sing "Found a Peanut" so gayly off-key that the others laughed.

Even Morann let a reluctant smile escape her.

Later, she managed to eat her share of the eggs and to nibble a piece of bannock.

When they had eaten and cleared away, Sarah pulled on a sweater and said, "It stays light beautifully long this far north, doesn't it? Let's just watch the shadows creep over the land. Let's just sit here for a while listening to the evening before anyone says a word."

It didn't sound too enticing to Morann. But neither did talking. When she had settled herself against her propped-up backpack, she closed her eyes and tried to blank out the whole world, natural and unnatural. Soon she was only vaguely aware of the cheepings and twitterings, of the little splashings in the lake. She was actually dozing off when a wild, unearthly laugh startled her.

She leaped up.

"It's only a loon," Sarah said, smiling reassuringly at her. "A big diving bird who seems to love lonely lakes. You know, there usually is a simple explanation for anything that seems uncanny. As she said that, she moved over and pulled Morann down beside her. "Morann, you're trembling."

"Well, I've had a bad day." Her voice cracked

a little on the "bad day."

"Of course you have. It's terrifying to be lost in the wilderness." Sarah put a firm arm around Morann and held her close for a minute before she said, "Suppose you tell us a bit about it."

"Well . . ." Morann started, and stopped. She shrugged with the hopelessness of trying to tell about Siem and the sea serpent and the foggy Band of Invisibles. But she tried again. "There was . . . There was a sky plume."

"Sky plume?" Kath flipped eagerly through her notebook. "Here it is: *Sky plume. Carried people away.* Remember, Sarah? That's all we could get out of him. *Sky plume. Carried people away.*" She narrowed her eyes and looked thoughtfully at her sister. "Morann. You heard me read my notes, didn't you?" Her voice was gentle.

"Well . . . of course."

Kath's sharp mind was homing right in on the facts. "Did your sky plume carry you away?"

"Well . . . sort of. Part of me. While the rest of me stayed leaning against a clump of heather."

"See! Well, don't you see, Morann? First you got lost. Well, you did get lost, didn't you?"

"Sort of, I guess. I . . . I didn't know where I was."

"And you sat down. By the clump of heather."

Sit down! And get on with it! Siem's imperious voice came back to her. "Yes. I . . . I sat down."

"Okay. Alone, lost, tired, you sat down; you leaned back against the heather. And, haunted by all the things you had heard, you fell asleep. Well?" All Kath demanded was a nice, simple, reasonable admission of a nice, simple, reasonable happening. "You were dreaming."

All right. Call it dreaming.

"Maybe. Sort of. But——" But it wasn't all nice and simple and reasonable like Kath thought.

"Let's just leave it at that," Sarah suggested, lifting a welcoming wave to Neil and Angus, who were hovering uncertainly about half way between the tents. She gestured for them to join the half circle facing the lake across the campfire.

"See any more *gigantopithecus* tracks?" Kath asked. Her eyes were on Angus.

But Neil answered. "Biggest thing we saw was a red squirrel with black stripes down its back."

Morann sat up alertly.

Kath was already sitting up. "Ogress squirrel," she declared.

"Ogress?" Morann scarcely breathed the word. Ogresses as well as sasquatches? She swallowed.

"Here it is." Kath pounced on the item: *"Ogress. Terrible old woman with teeth like wolf and claws like grizzly bear. Lured children into forest with basket of berries and ate them."*

"The kids or the berries?" asked Robin. "I know. She ate them together. Hey! You guys ought to put her on your team. Kids might taste better than caterpillars."

"Shut up, Robin!" Kath ordered. *"One day Ogress lured plump little Chief's son. Parents saw her clutch child. Too late for rescue. So they prayed to Great Spirit to save their child from her teeth and talons. Little redskin turned into red squirrel. Jumped out of her clutch. Ogress grabbed for him. Left four claw marks down his back.* And the moral is . . ."

"A squirrel in the pot should be eaten with berries," Robin suggested.

"You're hopeless," Kath told her, with a patient shrug towards Angus. "The moral is: Don't harm a red squirrel who has four stripes down his back!"

"Or . . . don't be tempted by berries!" Morann scarcely knew that she had said it until she saw everybody looking at her.

Sarah tightened her arm around Morann. "The moral is," she said brightly, "don't harm anything in the wilderness!"

"Not even an Ogress?" Robin objected. "An evil old Ogress!"

"Not even an Ogress. As far as I can make out, the basis of Indian belief is that nothing is evil in itself."

"Right," agreed Kath. "Nothing is evil in itself. But everything—everything and everybody —has the potential for good or harm. Everything! That's why you have to be so careful not to offend even a snail, or a tree, or——"

"Or an Ogress," Robin added.

"Let's change the subject," said Sarah, giving Morann a heartening squeeze.

An "Halloooooo!" changed it for them.

"It's a sasquatch," Robin guessed, straining to see what was coming along the trail towards them.

"Well, it sure ain't a gazelle," Neil agreed; he watched the heavy figure lumber its way.

"It's Joe," Kath announced positively. Angus's brother Joe. "He must be hard up for something to eat if he's coming to join the bug brigade."

Joe came puffing up to them, plump and good-natured and red in the face. "Hi savages," he greeted them. "Got any smoked moose left?" He flopped thankfully down before explaining why he had come. "Dad phoned, Angus. He's going to be home for one night before he disappears again into Darkest Scientifica. So Mom wants the genius to be home, too. You can come back here later, she said to tell you."

"Oh, that's okay," Angus assured him. "I'm not all that crazy about nature."

"You really haven't tried it with snail sauce," Robin told him in mock disapproval.

"We'll head home first thing in the morning," Joe went on. "Okay, guys?"

"Okay!" Neil's response was quick and enthu-siastic. Obviously he could see a polygraph coming up as well as a square meal.

"Okay." Angus glanced towards Kath and shrugged his shoulders.

Kath was apparently too busy flipping through her notebook to notice.

Joe threw off his light pack and rubbed his shoulders, then his legs. "I'm getting a trail bike for next time," he told them. "Walking is for jackasses." He rummaged around in his pack until he found some candy bars, which he tossed around the group.

"Joe! You're my favorite person," Robin screeched, tearing off a wrapper like someone who had been lost in the bush for three days.

"It's sure got dragonflies licked," Neil agreed, taking an appreciative nibble at his almond bar.

"Sorry about taking you away from the dragonflies, Neil," Angus said. "But maybe . . ." He glanced at Sarah to give her the chance to invite Neil to stay on and ride home with her.

"As a matter of fact," she countered, "I think we're all going home in the morning."

Kath and Robin howled their protests.

"Don't go home on my account," Morann said airily. "I've already decided that I'm going out with Joe and Angus. I'm not all that crazy about nature, either." And that was the truth. "So Neil can have my share of the pancakes and bacon."

"But——"

Sarah's objections were cut short by Robin.

"Joe's a very good driver, Sarah."

"So that's settled," Morann announced, taking a grim pleasure in the obvious relief of the girls. They were glad to get rid of her.

"Well . . ." Sarah couldn't really conceal her willingness to have Morann go home. "If you really do want to go home, dear . . ."

"I really do. And now you won't have to handcuff me."

"Oh . . ." Sarah waved off the very suggestion.

"Just tether me tonight and you'll be in the clear. Okay? Then that's settled. Good riddance to bad rubbish." She felt a fiendish delight in pursuing her misery.

"Never realized how good a bar was," Neil commented in a voice that was unusually loud for him. "I guess my pistons were getting a little sluggish on the fuel I was using."

"Have another tankful," Joe offered, digging out more bars.

"And how about some tea with it?" Sarah suggested, scrambling to her feet.

"Yeah. Let's celebrate!" Morann said. She didn't know why, but she wanted to flay everybody, including herself. *They* could celebrate getting rid of her. But what could she celebrate? Flunking the quest that might have made her wealthy? Achieving popularity zero? She felt Neil nudge her.

"I want to talk to you," he whispered.

"What about?" She eyed him with suspicion. But she got up and went with him along the edge of the lake.

"Hey, Neil!" Robin called after them. "Fasten her leash, eh?"

Neil ignored Robin. "Look!" Neil's voice was eager. "What is this about berries? And what's this about a stlalakum getting into you?"

"You don't have to believe me either."

"Who said I didn't believe you?"

"Well. Why should you? Nobody else does."

"You have to admit it's a little far out."

"So is plants wincing. So is plants knowing what you think, hundreds of miles away."

"Okay. Okay. Cool it."

"You cool it," Morann retorted. "Hey!" She stood stock still and looked at him. "Neil. You said that plants react emotionally, didn't you?"

"Well . . . yeah. So?"

"You also said 'but they've got nothing to feel with, nothing to think with.' Well, didn't you?"

"Yeah. So?"

"So!" Morann took a deep breath before coming out with a stupendous notion. "So!"

"Okay. Okay. So?"

"Plants *show* that they feel and think. Yet they've got nothing to feel with or think with. So! What's doing the feeling and the thinking?"

"You tell me."

"I will tell you. Stlalakums."

"Stlalakums?" Neil's immediate rejection of such a ridiculous idea gave way to an excited if reluctant consideration. "Hey! I guess you could have a point there."

She had another point, too, though she didn't know where the points were coming from all of a sudden. "You said maybe there's a cosmic communications system or something that animals and people-close-to-nature can tune in on—people like Indians used to be. Okay. What did Indians used to think when they were close enough to nature to tune in on your system?"

"You tell me."

"They thought there were spirits in the trees and things. Well, didn't they?"

"Well. Yeah. I guess so."

"Spirits. Stlalakum sprites. Invisibles. What's the difference?"

"Yeah." He seemed to consider it a possibility,

if a rather remote one.

"So!" She jumped in fast. "Why couldn't something get into me and make me wander off all alone? Do you honestly think I'm brave enough to go off into the wilderness alone?"

"You did go up Devil Mountain alone," he pointed out.

Morann sagged. "What's the use? I'm glad I'm going home. It'll be a relief to talk to somebody sensible like Gregory."

"Hey!" Neil warned her. "You'd better watch what you say to that kid. He's got a wild imagination . . . like his sister."

"Neil." Morann's voice became desperately earnest and quiet. "I wish I believed it was all just my wild imagination."

Neil looked at her. "You really do think something happened."

"What have I been saying? Something did happen to me. Something pretty scary."

"Hm."

"Hm yourself!" she retorted. "Honestly. I'm glad I'm going home even though———" Even though it meant that she had flunked the quest, that she had lost the only chance she'd ever have maybe to be rich and important.

"Even though . . .?"

"Even though I have to inflict myself on Joe and Angus," she said fiercely. Talk about zero popularity! At least she wasn't popular with

Siem either, nor with the scary Voices. They wouldn't bother her any more. They'd decide, all of them, that she wasn't worth their trouble. "I just hope——"

"You just hope what?"

"I just hope I never hear about your psycho-galvanised whatever-it-was again as long as I live. That's what started it all. Your crazy article in *Wildlife*."

"It wasn't a crazy article, Morann. It was a scientific fact."

"Well, so is what happened to me. A scientific fact. Even if nobody's figured out yet about that kind of science."

"Okay. Okay. I believe you."

"How can you believe me when you don't know what happened?"

"You could tell me what happened."

"Huh! I've got enough people now thinking I've blown my mind."

They were standing under a tree—about the only tree that had no branches close to the ground. And now they stood silent in the silence of the evening, watching nighthawks swoop and dip, catching insects on the wing.

WHAP.

Something dropped down on Neil. Something big and dark and heavy.

Morann screamed.

"Gotcha!" Robin yelled in triumph before Neil

threw her off in a flailing fury of arms and legs.

"What's happened?" Everybody was rushing towards them.

"Robin!" Sarah was aghast. "How could you do such a thing when you know Morann is upset?"

"I'm sorry, but—— Oh, Sarah, I thought this was going to be a fun campout."

"It will be as soon as you get rid of me," Morann told her shrilly.

"Robin, the water's boiling," Kath said firmly. "You make that tea!"

They drank the tea with feeble attempts at making it a celebration, a farewell-to-the-grubs celebration. But the immense silences of the mountains kept pressing in on them.

A coyote howled somewhere away off in the hills. And another coyote answered him in the high, long-drawn-out call of the wild. Then a loon laughed his unearthly laugh away off on a lonely lake.

Morann shivered. All the eerie things were still out there, silently waiting in the great Stlalakum Wild.

"We've all had a big day," Sarah announced, scrambling to her feet. "I suggest we turn in."

"I don't suppose you're planning any little safari tonight, Morann?" Kath inquired; and she tried to make it sound joking.

"I'm not. But tie me to the tent pole anyway."

Not that it would do any good. Your smistiux couldn't be tied down. "Tie me!" she challenged. If they wouldn't believe the truth, then they might as well believe that she was a fearless, swashbuckling adventurer. She might as well be something instead of a real nothing. A real, absolute goose egg, zero, nothing.

Morann blinked back sudden hot tears and fled into the tent. It was even worse to be a nothing when you had had the chance to be rich and famous and popular, with your name and your picture in the paper, and people crowding around you to ask questions about your fantastic adventures.

"I wish the voices *would* come back," she muttered fiercely under her breath. "Even if . . . even if it meant that they all got rid of me forever."

10

THE VOICES DIDN'T COME BACK. THEY HAD ALL GIVEN up on a goop like her.

Morann sensed the lovely lift of morning in the mountain meadows. Light mists were rising from the lake. Birds tilted their heads back to send their songs upward.

Yet her own spirits seemed to be caught in a downdraft. Her big chance had come, and gone.

"Flapjacks before you go, Morann," Sarah decreed.

"Flapjacks coming right up," Kath agreed briskly.

"With magnificent hydrated dehydrated syrup,"

Robin added, hoisting the collapsible water bucket.

Everyone was noticeably nice to her. And she didn't know why she accepted their pleasantries with such chill dignity.

When she'd had breakfast and the boys seemed ready to move out, she shouldered her backpack.

"See you," she said as casually as she could.

"Stick to Joe!" Kath admonished her in a whisper.

"Don't hitch a ride with any Flying Feather!" Robin boomed out.

Flying Feather? Of course. Since she had never actually described the sky plume, they visualized her clinging to the end of a big, magical feather. No wonder they thought she was making it all up.

"If I do, Robin," she retorted, "I'll try to arrange it so I can drop down right on you." Head high, she stalked off towards the trail, leaving the boys to follow.

"Hey, Morann! Wait up!" Joe called after her. "This isn't a race."

Actually, she was glad to wait so that she could march in the middle every step of the way. But she made it look as if she were lingering to watch the rhythmically dipping flight of a tiny goldfinch. With his warble and his color, he seemed like a wild canary celebrating his wildness.

"It's really great up here, isn't it?" she heard Neil saying over her shoulder. "Too bad you're leaving."

"Glad someone thinks so," she answered. And she leaned forward, interested in a low bush that she could scarcely see for the rush of hot tears.

As they moved out along the trail, though, her spirits began to lift a little. Joe's good-natured complaints about walking heightened her own sense of agility. She felt the spring in her own steps.

"It's all right for you," he told her, stopping to rest about a quarter of a mile along. "You move like a squirrel . . . like a squirrel following a hedgehog," he added in self-deprecation.

She felt a warm surge of liking for big, lumbering Joe.

"I'm sure going to hit Dad up tonight for a trail bike," he said the next time he stopped for a breather. It'd be really great, zooming along here on a trail bike."

Joe liked machines. He liked cars. And as Robin had noted, he was a very good driver. After a hot dog at the service station counter at the end of the trail, he took them down the twisting highway with quiet skill.

He slowed near a lake resort to ply Morann with offers of ice cream? a shake? a hamburger? coke? "Sure you wouldn't like something?"

"I'm sure, Joe. But thanks just the same." She really did not want any more to eat. But it was nice to be treated like someone special. Morann found herself wishing the miles would stretch out.

She was genuinely sorry when they turned into her street.

"Just drop me off at the front, Joe," she suggested. "And thanks a million. Nicest ride I ever had. You should give Mom driving lessons."

"Any time you need a lift," he urged her. "And when I get the trail bike, you get the first ride."

"I'll hold you to that," she told him. Then she got out, took her backpack from Angus's long, skinny hands, and waited until they drove off. "Thanks again," she called after them. "And don't forget about the bike ride!"

Then it hit her for the first time. What was she going to tell Mom? Her warm glow faded, her shoulders sagged. She hefted her pack and swung it thoughtfully. What was she going to tell Mom?

"Oh, I'll think of something," she muttered. And, squaring her shoulders, she marched to the back door.

The back door was locked. The house was quiet.

Nobody was home over at Neil's place either. Probably they had all gone off shopping together.

Morann flopped down in a garden chair. "Well!" What a homecoming! Nobody knew, or cared, where she was. Her gaze ranged over the garden. And suddenly its strange quietness struck her. There didn't seem to be a bee buzzing or a bird chirping. There wasn't a breath of air stirring the leaves of the shade trees. It was as if everything were silently waiting.

Morann swallowed. What was everything waiting for?

"Me?" It came out in a scared little whisper. Here she was, alone again. No matter what she did, it seemed to turn out that way. And this time, as before, everybody thought she was safely with someone else. No one would worry about her or go out looking for her. It was as if everything had been arranged, once again.

Morann grabbed both arms of the chair. Then she relaxed her grip. What was the use of hanging on? If they took you, they took you. You could not escape them.

Still, Kath had said that everything had potential for harm or good. Maybe even her aloneness didn't have to be a bad thing. She wasn't helpless, was she? In fact . . . since nobody knew that she wasn't safely with someone else, she was free to ——to do what?

The garden was still hushed and waiting.

It did seem as if everything had been arranged! To give her a second chance at the quest? To give her a second chance to find—— To find what? The gold maybe? A second chance to prove that she was something besides a dead loss.

Morann jumped to her feet. Rushing to commit herself to the venture before she could think, she filled her water canteen from the garden tap. She glanced about to see that she hadn't dropped a telltale kerchief or a gum wrapper. Then she slung on the backpack and scooted out of the garden. With any luck, she'd catch the early afternoon bus.

No matter which way you looked at it, she was doing the only sensible thing, she told herself as she sprinted down back lanes and side streets to reach a sensibly distant bus stop.

Sooner or later, Sarah and the girls would have to decide whether Morann was a sulky, snivelling freak or a courageous adventurer. If she had anything to do with it, she intended to be a courageous adventurer.

And Mom? Well, this would keep her from thinking that her youngest daughter had been sent home from the hills in disgrace, which is what Mom would think no matter how much Morann insisted that she had volunteered to come home. Why had she volunteered? Mom would ask. And the why would only start her worrying about Morann's imagination the way she already worried about Gregory's. Simply not appearing was the kindest thing she could do for her mother.

And Siem? Morann narrowed her eyes and squashed her mouth shut. Siem thought she was unworthy. "Well! We'll see about that," she muttered.

Actually, this quest wasn't going to worry anybody, because everybody thought she was safely with somebody else. And in the end, when she breezed in with her treasure, whatever it was, it was going to be fabulous for the whole family. Like winning the gold brick door-prize at the Pacific National Exhibition. Morann had a glimpse of herself as the hero of the family. Her picture would be in the paper. And on TV. Everyone would be crowding around to get her to sign autograph albums.

Stepping aboard the cross-valley bus with her neat backpack, Morann wouldn't have aroused the suspicions of the sharpest-eyed little old lady. She even had the exact fare ready, since Mom had given her holiday money and there had been no place to spend it in the alpine meadows. She got off at Wayne's Corner as nonchalantly as you would get off a school bus at your own stop. And she stepped briskly along the country road towards Devil Mountain.

It was cooler this time, more comfortable for walking. And she wasn't even hungry. Which was fortunate, since there was nothing to eat in her backpack. After being so scornfully dismissed by Siem, she obviously had to prove herself worthy of being reinstated in the quest. And those Indian children of the "good old days" had evidently fasted when they went off alone into the hills to seek their fortune. Well, anything they could do, she could do better.

Morann squared her shoulders and stepped along. What was so bad about going up Devil Mountain in the broad daylight? And what was so terrible about spending one night up there? As long as she kept her mind on the treasure at the end of the quest, like the heroes in the stories, she'd make it. People on a quest always made it.

She reached the edge of the woods, where the trail started. This time there was no familiar car parked there. In fact, there was no car at all; apparently people didn't hike up Devil Mountain on a day like Thursday.

There, at the edge of the wilderness, she hesitated, tempted to turn and run. She could turn back without loss of face. Nobody knew what she had planned to do, so nobody would know that she had failed to do it. Except Morann, herself. She sighed deeply and closed her eyes for a moment. Then she slipped swiftly into the woods.

Actually, as before it was very pleasant just beyond the dusty edge. Wild pea vine still made green and blue patterns under the cool alders. And again Morann noticed how beautiful they were with their clusters of tiny sweet peas perched as lightly as butterflies along the fragile, green stems. She leaned over to smell the delicate fragrance.

A bee hurtled off. She was an intruder, disturbing those who belonged. So she moved a little more timidly on into the deeper, darker forest.

The mountain path was so narrow and so seldom used that salmonberry bushes seemed to be holding out their arms across it, trying to make her go back.

Morann pushed past them as inoffensively as she could. And she almost toed in, Indian fashion, to keep from crushing salal with her feet; for, close to the ground, its leathery green leaves seemed to be trying to reclaim the wilderness. This was salal, she realized; those berries had been something else.

Deeper in the woods, the ferns took over. They spouted up from the earth in vigorous fountains, luminous green where the sun filtered through to them, brooding and dark where the trees' shadows fell across them. She could smell the ferns. Or perhaps it was the moist earth she could smell, and the dark slugs hiding there, watching her. She could sense the worms crawling along through the loose forest floor, turning everything back into wilderness. She could feel the woods' rejection of her. If she fell and couldn't get up, everything there would work to silently cover her over until they silently turned her, too, into quiet green growth.

Moving on through a stand of tall timber, she stopped to rest a moment. As she glanced up, she sensed something rushing upward on all sides, surging upward towards the free air. The strong upward surge made her dizzy. Catching at a bush, she crashed through it into a decaying log, smashing countless little green things. "Oh dear!" she gasped, aghast to have offended any part of the powerful plant world.

When she picked herself up, she found her fingers trailing a dark, root-fringed string of small green leaves and tiny pink twin flowers. The flowers trembled in pairs on stems that were as thin as a thread, yet as upstanding as toothpicks. "I'm sorry," she told them. And rather than just throw them down to die, she twined them around her head. "Queen Morann," she announced, trying to be blithe about it. But Queen Morann scrambled on up Devil Mountain in a highly unregal manner.

She was thankful to emerge finally into the airy brightness of the lookout rock.

"Phew!" she said, flopping down on the warmed rock. She looked out over the valley below. The farmhouses seemed so snug and safe in their nests of shade trees. The farms seemed so secure with their fences and their big barns and their cows grazing along the streams where the poplars grew. And here and there a flash of red or yellow was a tractor busy with the sensible, clattering, open-air work of the farmers.

Morann leaned back against a warm stone. It had been a big day. And there was no hurry. There was no use getting up to that lonely little lake any earlier than she had to. She closed her eyes to bask in the pleasant heat of the afternoon sun. There was still a stiff climb ahead of her, so she might as well be rested.

Slowly the warmth relaxed Morann. The world

grew drowsy and quiet.

"Siem was wrong." The high voice drifted into her consciousness so gently that she did not even open her eyes. "I knew Siem was wrong. The "Siem" and the "wrong" were long-drawn-out wails.

The deeper voice almost agreed. "It does seem so." The words drifted to Morann "seeeeeeeeem soooooooooooo."

"She is looking back at the place she came from. Let her look even farther back!" "Farther" was a long, long word that seemed to stretch into another time.

Though her eyes must still be closed, Morann saw the valley spread out below her: the familiar prairieland, the creeks with the poplar trees, the river, and the mountains beyond the river. But it was not the same. High grasses waved free, freer than Morann had ever seen grasses wave. And mixed among the waving grasses were wild flowers, and deer grazing here and there. Close to the river it was like a fair, a holiday encampment. Indian lodges stood in the sunshine. They were Indian people with bright feathers and shells in their hair and decoration glinting on their clothing. Their painted canoes were drawn up by the river.

The roundfish harvest. The words came to Morann. From Kath's notebook? *The roundfish harvest.* These people had gathered from far up and down the river. They were waiting for the roundfish run; and they were enjoying themselves while they waited. They were enjoying the lovely prairie. Their tom-toms reached her, and their singing. She sensed that the very mountains were listening to the music of these people who belonged here, like the deer. These Indian people who had lived here thousands and thousands of years and still kept the land lovely.

"Ch-ach-a-t-ch!"

Morann leaped up, startled. But it was only the squirrel. The Ogress squirrel. The black stripes down his back were the claw marks of the Ogress.

"Hi, squirrel," she said, in what was barely a whisper.

She glanced back at the valley. And there were the farmhouses, snug in their nests of shade trees. There were the fences, the fields, the barns, and the tractors.

Morann swallowed. And pushing back her hair, she discovered her garland. "Poor little flowers!" They were limp now; their delicate pink perkiness was gone. The stems lay as limp as rubber bands. All the vitality was gone. What was this vitality that lay at the base of life? When it left, only a wilted lifelessness remained. A sadness.

"I'm sorry," she said softly.

"Ch-ach-a-t-ch!"

"Okay. Okay. I'm coming."

Morann took a long, deep breath and closed her eyes prayerfully for a moment. Then she went on up Devil Mountain, into the deeper woods.

She was going to see this thing through.

11

WHEN SHE HAD COME DOWN THE MOUNTAINSIDE with the girls, Morann had not noticed the trail as she had going up, the trail through the deeper, darker woods. But now she saw once again all the fallen timbers, rotting away under their shrouds of green moss. Their pale fungi seemed once more like ghostly ears straining to listen for unnatural movement. She found herself straining to listen with them in the overwhelming silence of the forest. But even her own footfalls were quiet on the moist, yielding earth. All sound seemed to be sinking away into the silencing mosses that covered logs and rocks and roots in the deep woods.

How could you know what awful movements they were muffling?

Crack.

The snap of a twig in all that awful silence was as startling as a rifle shot. Morann stopped and held her breath. But there was no more sound. She let her breath out carefully. Waiting and listening, she sensed that something else was waiting, too, and listening in the forest behind her. Yet all sound seemed to be sinking away into the deep, deep green mosses, leaving only silence.

A light rain began to fall, so light that it seemed as if the world of the woods was silently weeping.

Then she noticed the Indian pipes glimmering in the dark woods like tiny ghosts. Translucent white, they seemed to be the ghosts of dead flowers, watching her, waiting to see if she were good or evil. Even while she wished she could reach out and touch them to convince herself that they were solid plants, her mind shrank from the contact. What if her hand moved right through them, as it would move through a mist?

She fled on up the rough trail, twisting and ducking to keep her backpack from snagging. And when she tripped on a root, she found her hand only inches away from a group of strange little flowers that seemed to have been posted there, like the ghostly pipes, to keep an eye on her passage. Though beautifully bell-shaped, they were a ghastly yellow-green, spotted with the color of dried blood. And the tip of each split pistil was like a flicked-out snake's tongue. "Once you were evil little reptiles," she heard herself mutter. And she gasped. Where had such a thought come from? Morann scrambled to her feet and rushed on up the mountain. What an awful thing to have said to little flowers! She fled in fear of some eerie retaliation.

The light rain stopped, leaving a mist moving through the highest trees. Or was it a mist? Could it be a Band of Invisibles trailing their robes and veils along the tree tops, keeping an eye on her?

The trail forked. She hadn't noticed the fork before, when she was coming down the mountain. The need for a choice of ways alarmed her. What if she chose the wrong one and found herself moving into one of those huge, rugged mountains behind Devil Mountain?

The left fork seemed to swing around the mountain, while the right one went almost straight up. So she chose the right fork. But she still didn't feel sure. Terrified that it might be the wrong choice, Morann rushed and tripped and stumbled up.

Then, suddenly, she came out at the stunted, twisted cedars. She had almost forgotten about them. But there they were again, their branches like droopy arms and like droopy heads wrapped in shawls, their trunks twisted round and round. And maybe there were old, old bones lying somewhere below them.

The Seexqi.

She could not keep the Seexqi out of her thoughts one minute longer. If she saw the Seexqi, she must not turn and run away, no matter how horrifying. She must not turn and run. *If you ever turned your back on that animal, you would start to spin round till you were dizzy. And you would go out of your mind. Or drop dead.*

Morann swallowed. She couldn't keep her eyes from looking at those twisted tree trunks. Why on earth had she gone on such a mad quest? Why hadn't she just stayed at home in the garden? Why hadn't she just taken the key from its hiding place near the back door, gone in, and waited for Mom to get back from her shopping?

She waited a long, long time near the cedars, getting courage to go on to the deep, dark lake that had a subterranean channel connecting it with the open sea, a channel that could suck her in.

Finally she sat down to think things over. Actually, she could stay right where she was and avoid the scarier prospects. She was glancing around for a sleeping spot when her gaze fell on some berries. They were exactly the same kind of berries; and they fascinated her the way a snake fascinates a watching bird.

She went over to look at them more closely. Yes, they were exactly the same as the ones she

had eaten before, the berries that had caused all the trouble. Fearfully, she picked a small handful and then sat looking at them.

Suddenly she gulped them down. It was all or nothing on this trip up Devil Mountain. And then, sensing that she was committed in some way she did not understand, she got to her feet and headed for Stlalakum Lake.

That was where it was going to happen.

The lake was even darker than before, with the long, long shadows of evening turning it a deeper, gloomier green. It seemed almost as if the shadow-spirits of the crowding trees were slipping down into the lake for a meeting with the Seexqi, leaving the surface empty and silent, more empty and silent than anything she had ever known. The silence had a waitingness in it. Something was going to happen. Something awful and stlalakum.

Eyes no bigger than black beads were watching her. And she realized that they were the eyes of a tiny, dark salamander with a form as old as the Age of Reptiles. What was it thinking?

Suddenly it darted into the edge of the lake, as though it had gone to report her presence to a deep meeting of reptiles and shadows.

Morann gasped. What were they planning away down there? Deep down there where a subterranean channel led out to the open sea.

She slipped off her pack and let it down to the ground carefully, quietly. Almost holding her breath, she unbuckled it and took out a sweater, which she silently put on. It was cold at Stlalakum Lake, with the coldness of waiting reptiles.

Again she felt beady eyes watching her from the dark earth. And this time she caught the slither of a snake. It too disappeared into the lake.

What was happening at the meeting down there?

She scanned the evening sky, almost hoping for a small, high cloud stretching out into a beautiful white plume as it moved down towards her. But there was nothing.

Yet something was going to happen. It had to. So she had better get ready for it. Biting her lower lip in her efforts to move in silence, Morann unstrapped her bedroll. Where should she spread out her groundsheet? What space was free of snails and slugs and salamanders and snakes? She tiptoed cautiously both ways from the lone alder tree, whose low branches reached out over the blackening water. Actually, a spot near its trunk seemed the likeliest place. It was awfully close to the lake, of course; but the branches gave a certain screened, protected feeling. And anyway, if she moved any distance at all from the water, she would be awfully close to the gloom of the forest.

As quietly as she could, Morann spread out the groundsheet and sleeping bag. When that was done, she found herself shivering. So she took out her light zippered jacket-with-hood and put it on too, on top of the sweater.

Who knew how soon it would happen? Perhaps she ought to just get into her sleeping bag and wait motionless. She'd keep her head towards the woods and her feet towards the water. That way, she could scramble out, away from the first ripple that broke the surface if it seemed too terrifying. But she must move backwards. She must not turn and run. *If you ever turned your back on that animal, you would start to spin round till you were dizzy. And you would go out of your mind. Or drop dead.*

The trees were watching her, waiting to see what she would do. She could feel them watching and waiting.

When it did happen, whatever it, was, what if she were so terrified that she leaped up in horror and tripped into the lake and went down, down, down to where the channel would suck her in?

Perhaps she should tie the roll-up tapes of her

sleeping bag to an alder branch. Then at least she wouldn't tumble into the water while she was scrambling to her feet. But the tapes weren't all that strong, she noticed. One terrified tug might rip them off. Her eyes lighted on the climbing rope that had been snapped on to her borrowed backpack. That would be better. With it, she could anchor herself, bag and all.

The increasing darkness of the lake fascinated her strangely. She could feel it pulling her mind the way it might pull her body, down, down, down to the subterranean channel. Perhaps the sea serpent was an evil lure, waiting out there at the ocean end of the channel.

Wrenching her thoughts away from the lake, Morann slipped into the sleeping bag. Then, zippering it up as far as her chest, she sat up to fix the rope. First she circled it around her and the bag. Then she tied it to a thick branch. But was that a good square knot? she wondered; or was it a granny that would slip just when she needed it? Morann scowled at it anxiously and tied several extra knots. It was better to be safe than sorry.

After taking a good swig of water from her canteen, she stretched out and zippered the sleeping bag shut. She was thankful that it zippered up tightly around her neck. Just to be safe, working from the inside, she gave the zipper a couple of sharp tugs sideways to be sure it would stay shut. She tried not to notice how grindingly, gurglingly empty she was.

Then it really hit her. Nobody in the whole wide world knew where she was. Anything could happen to her and nobody would ever know. She could be lying there bleeding to death from poison fangs, and nobody would send in a search-and-rescue party. It was such a terrifying thought that Morann tried to push it out of her mind with thoughts of what she would do with a treasure, if treasure there was. She'd buy a summer cabin for the family, and a boat with an outboard motor and water skis. She made herself envision the cabin and the outboard motor and the water skiing. Kath would be competent on the skis, but Robin would keep acting crazy.

She must have dozed off. Certainly when her eyes next opened, the world was surprisingly dark. Morann only realized how very dark it was when she saw two eyes glowing at her from the darkness of the forest. Animal eyes? Or a sasquatch? *They can see in the dark. Their eyes glow like cats' eyes.* Why, oh why was Kath so good at getting facts down in neat notes? And why did she insist on reading them to the family?

Well. The only way to get rid of those awful, waiting eyes was to shut her own. She would not look.

Crack. She heard the snap of a branch, from near the eyes. So she pressed her sleeping bag over her ears. She would not listen, either.

She didn't know why she opened her eyes again, for the alarming apparition she saw then was as silent as a ghost slipping through the trees. It floated through the air, eerily bright against the dark forest. It was like a big owl, utterly soundless, frighteningly luminous. It swooped down. Became a part of some creature's tiny scream. And slipped away through the forest.

Morann's heart was pounding. She could not have seen that. It must have been a nightmare. But she knew it wasn't. She had seen the apparition. And scarcely daring to breathe, she once more pulled the sleeping bag up over her eyes and ears. She'd never go to sleep again.

Fortunately her day had been long and exhausting. And she did fall asleep again.

"Kwyaaaaak. Kwyaaaaak."

Her eyes flew open. Moonlight silvered the silent world of Stlalakum Lake, giving it an unearthly sheen, a ghostly lightness. Nothing seemed real or solid.

"Kwyaaaaak Kwyaaaaak."

That sounded so terribly real and solid that Morann jammed her eyes shut and pulled the top of her sleeping bag up over her head. If you wouldn't look, then you wouldn't see it—the Seexqi.

Makes a noise like a duck, but much, much louder.

The terrifying stlalakum serpent must be raising his two heads, there where the two cries had come from. Praying that she looked like a mossy green log half hidden by alder branches, Morann held herself stiff and still as any fallen timber in the forest. And she felt as crumbling away inside.

"Kwyaaaaak. Kwyaaaaaak."

In spite of herself, she peeped out.

A dreadful reptilian head was raised high above the water, not far from the end of the alder branches. But it wasn't looking at her. It was looking across the moonlit lake at another terrible reptilian head raised high above the water.

Morann sat up in sheer shock, bag and all.

If you saw that animal, you would not dare to turn round and run.

Wouldn't you? Morann had news for Kath's Indian informants. She sprang up; but fell back down, thwarted by the rope with its triple knots. Did that awful head turn a trifle to listen?

Frantic to escape, she felt for the pull tab on her zipper, to free her arms to cope with the granny knots. But it wouldn't pull. The sideways tugs she had given it had done something. Half sobbing, she yanked at it. But it wouldn't give. She couldn't get her arms out.

Now one reptilian head seemed to be closer, almost towering over her. Its fangs glinted; its awful tongue flicked out. If it flicked her way, it might even reach her. But she could not escape. Faint with horror, Morann shut her eyes and pressed the sleeping bag against them. She did not want to see the moment when the awful head turned and saw her. Once more she held herself stiff as a log, scarcely daring to breathe.

She heard a thrashing of water.

Terror opened her eyes.

The Seexqi was gone. The lake was wild with waves. And it seemed to Morann that she could see a darker darkness undulating, down, down, down towards the subterranean channel.

But it could come back. She had to get away in case it came back. So she yanked frantically at the zipper until it gave. Then, weak with relief, she flopped back for a moment. She *had* seen the Seexqi. It had not been just her imagining. The lake was still shivering.

She caught her breath at a sudden dimming of the moonlight.

But it was only a mist that passed over the moon. It was a high, small cloud, swiftly moving towards her. And as it came down, it stretched out into a great plume of cloud. The shaft of the feather was moving towards Stlalakum Lake.

As motionless as if caught in a spell, Morann watched it touch down.

The feathery cloud was a million tiny Invisibles, trailing wisps of gossamer veiling as they darted and swooped in endless restlessness.

The night was not over.

12

STILL MOTIONLESS, MORANN HEARD THE FAMILIAR voices.

"What did I tell you?" The higher voice was jubilant. "I knew it. I knew it. This child is on the old, old quest." The words were filled with longing. "And now she has met the first test. She has faced the Seexqi; and she has not turned and run away."

"True," the deeper voice agreed. "She has not turned and run away. She is braver than I thought."

"Braver?" Morann muttered. Then she bit her tongue. If they thought she was brave, fine. Admiration was a nice change. Unless her "bravery" encouraged them to swoop her off to another, worse test. Maybe out to the sea serpent.

One moment Morann was lying there, listening to the voices from the foggy feather.

The next she was gazing down at her own inert body, tied into its green bag like a sack of old bones. If she never got back, it would turn into a sack of old bones. And no one might ever know.

"Do not think failure, Morann!"

"Siem!"

There was the gleam of pearly robes, shifting and shimmering in the moonlight in an ever-changing pattern of squared ovals.

"Your voices insist that you are worthy, Morann. They say you did not turn and run away from the Seexqi. They say you held fast."

"Well . . . Well, I . . . I didn't run away." Maybe she could stick to simple facts the way Kath did.

"Obviously not." Siem's tone suggested that the Stlalakum chief was willing to go along with the technical meeting of conditions. In Morann's case, that would have to do.

"Where are you taking me?" To face the sea serpent? Or to see where the treasure was?

"To see where the treasure is," Siem answered. "It shows how desperate we are becoming these days."

"Desperate?"

"How many offers do you think we are receiving these days?" he asked her, almost sadly.

"Offers?" Somehow, whenever she was talking to Siem, Morann's part of the conversation was not exactly scintillating. "Offers of what?"

"Of bodies."

"Bodies?" What did that mean? Such as it was, she treasured her body. She really didn't want to lose it.

"If we had bodies of our own, do you think we would need to use yours?"

"But——you're not using mine." It was lying there like a bag of old bones.

"Not at the moment, thank the Wisdom of the Wild."

"What's the Wisdom of the Wild?"

"Nothing that is likely to involve you very deeply." Siem was worse than Kath was at putting Morann down. "Still, we do have to use what we can get when——"

"When you've shown me where the treasure is?" Morann interrupted. Invisibles wouldn't make much of a work force when it came to digging a treasure out, mining gold maybe.

"You do like that word treasure," Siem's voice held a thundering sort of threat. "I suppose you do realize, Morann, that the treasure you talk of so lightly has been patiently built up over millions of years?"

"Really?" Then it must be an enormous treasure.

"It is an enormous treasure." The thunder broke and rumbled through the strangely powerful small voice. A shimmering gesture drew Morann's attention to the land they were passing over.

Moonlight had transformed the mountains. It had given them an otherworldly beauty, a beauty that had been building up for a million years. Now where did that thought come from? she wondered. Then she realized that it was just an echo of Siem's words.

She did not know exactly where she was until she saw the tent, the yellow tent beside the small lake. They were coming down in the alpine meadows.

The sky plume hovered over the silent camp. Then slowly it drifted on to the little creek that flowed into the lake, near the tents, and followed its glistening turns upstream towards its mother mountain. The plume traced the stream around a mound of silvered-blue lupine, then around a grove of alpine fir trees, and on towards a big rock outcropping. And there the misty band swooped very low, so low that Morann could see a bank of golden flowers that seemed to be opening wide in welcome to Siem. As if a breeze were passing over them, they seemed to bow towards the sky plume.

A bank of golden flowers! "This is where the treasure is," she said, with sudden knowing.

"This is where the treasure is," Siem agreed.

Then, with a shimmering gesture, the Respected Person whisked Morann up and away from thoughts of gold.

The sky plume lifted fast, over the moonlit meadows, back over the shadowy mountains.

Morann caught the dark glint of Stlalakum Lake. It was like highly polished slate, framed by dark trees. They were taking her back to the terrible, bottomless waters.

One minute she was looking down at her inert body tied to the alder branch like a bag of old bones.

The next minute—or it seemed the next minute —a flash of light on her eyes woke her up from a sound sleep. It was a glint of sun through the alder branches. And birds were twittering.

It was morning. Morann couldn't believe it. She had survived.

Then the full glory of her survival hit her. "And I know where the gold is." It must be gold. "I'm sure it's gold," she whispered.

Morann sat up, carefully working the zipper down. At the bottom she saw it—the rope end lying like the great S of a serpent on her sleeping bag. And as if to indicate that this was a sea serpent's sign, the tapes of the sleeping bag had been dribbled along the curving rope like the wave pattern Gregory made with blue crayons when he drew sailboats with ducks' feet.

She caught her breath. The sign of the sea ser-

pent could not be on *Her*.

Then she sagged with relief. It wasn't the awful sign. When she looked at it now, she could see that it was more like a dollar sign, a glorious sign for the girl who knew where the gold was hidden. It was the sign of her fortune. A sign that she would be rich.

Morann wriggled up out of the bag and got to work on the knots that had held her fast to the alder. She was eager to get home where the food was. She was desperately hungry. And scrounge as she might through her pack, she could not find so much as a solitary raisin. "Fridge, here I come," she sang out as she snapped the climbing rope onto her backpack.

Morann went down the mountainside so fast that her knees were trembling before she reached the bottom. But they weren't trembling with fear. The woods weren't so awful in the bright, early morning. Birds twittered along the trail, and squirrels scampered about. The ferns seemed almost golden green. They reminded her of a bank of golden flowers. Her mind was full of golden dreams, of golden plans for the future.

The whole adventure had been a triumph. She was about to be rich. She was about to be the hero of the entire Fenn family.

In the meantime, though, she had to wait for her cross-valley bus for over an hour, while she perished with impatience. Still, she reached home before lunch.

"Morann!" Mom said as she walked in through the back door. "I thought you were going to stay in the mountains till Monday morning."

"The rest are. But I got a lift out with Angus and Joe."

"You're all right? You're not hurt?"

"Of course not, Mom."

"Must be Homecoming Day," Mom observed. "Dad just phoned. He's coming home tonight."

Tonight? Just in time to get her back up into the meadows! As if it were all arranged, again. She didn't realize that she was standing with her mouth open until her mother spoke.

"What is it?"

"Oh, I . . . I guess I'm psychic." Without giving her mother a chance to ask another question, Morann plunged headlong into some instant plans. "I guess I must have known Dad would

come home. Something made me come home."
That was sort of true, wasn't it? She plunged on.
"Mom! Since Sarah has to head home Wednes-
day, and since Dad has had no chance to see her,
and since it would be absolutely fabulous to have
a family picnic up there in the alpine meadows,
let's go! I didn't tell the others I'd be coming
back with a surprise party. They just thought I
wanted to go home. Mom, couldn't we go there
first thing tomorrow morning? And couldn't we
make a special cake with gold icing and—"

"Hold it! Hold it!" Mom said. But Morann
could see that she liked the whole idea. "Dad has
a few things to do tomorrow, but we could plan
for Sunday."

"Okay. Sunday. It's all set." Morann hoped
she wouldn't die of despair waiting for Sunday
to get there.

"Morann!" It was Gregory.

She caught him up. "Gwuggelly, we're all going up into the alpine meadows on Sunday. And
you'll love it. You'll love it."

Things were working out just too beautifully.
Morann kept crossing her fingers behind her
back. She kept closing her eyes in a sort of pray-
erful thinking.

Nobody in the whole wide world suspected
her overnight stlalakum adventure. So the whole
business of finding gold was going to stun them.
And not until then would she tell the whole fan-

tastic story. How could they not believe her then? When she held the proof in her hands.

From then on it would be she, and not Kath's neat notes, who would be consulted for stlalakum information. And when Sarah came back next year to do some real research, who would have to be the one who went everywhere with Sarah?

She could see them all, Sunday, crowding around her near that bank of golden flowers when she was filling them with the story. She could just see their faces as they heard about Siem and the sky plume and the Band of Invisibles and the sea serpent and the Seexqi. And how could they not believe her? Then, when they had seen the gold.

Again and again and again, Morann jammed her eyes shut to visualize the exact route from the yellow tent by the lake to the bank of golden flowers surrounding the rock outcropping. She had never gone that way on the ground. So, the moment she began to see the landmarks—the mound of blue lupine, the grove of alpine firs, the big rock outcropping—she'd be able to stop pinching herself. She'd know for sure that it was all true.

And if the landmarks weren't there?

But they had to be there. And Morann thought she'd go mad waiting for Sunday to prove it. They had to be there. Whenever she was sure no one was watching, she flung her arms wide and leaped about like a ballet dancer. She dreamed up a gloriously wild ballet called *Morann's Millions*.

Having a geologist father was part of the every-thing that was working out just too perfectly. He would know exactly what to do, once she had shown him where the gold was. He was even a very good photographer. And that, too, could be worked in. She could get every last little thing set up without anyone suspecting what she was about to spring on them.

Only one little thing ever brought her up short. Why?

Why had Siem shown her where the treasure was? Clearly disapproving of Morann, always ready to whisk her up and away from any mention of gold, Siem was "desperate" to use a body. They needed a body. To dig up the gold? But why?

One possibility occurred to her. Was something going to happen as soon as she had brought up the treasure? Was the sky plume going to swoop down to take it?

No, she assured herself. The sky plume couldn't lift anything heavier than a smistiux.

Another wild thought alarmed her. Was the Seexqi going to slither up and take the gold to the lake and let it gurgle down, down, down and out through the subterranean channel to the waiting sea serpent? Was it gold that the sea serpent was after? Siem had called him greedy. Did the stla-lakums want to get gold for him so he'd go away?

Morann kept pushing such mad thoughts away from her mind. A treasure was a treasure. It was not the lure of the sea serpent or something horrible like that. She busied her brains with working out a wildly joyous finale for *Morann's Millions*. Yet—why were they doing this? Why was Siem desperate?

There was nothing sinister about it, she told herself firmly. By some strange chance, she had gone alone to a stlalakum lake and had eaten a mysterious kind of berry; and by that chance she, Morann Fenn, had become part of a quest and the rightful owner of a treasure. Just the way primitive tribes had often accepted an ordinary, fair-haired, shipwrecked man or woman as the golden-haired god or godess they had been expecting. That was the why.

Still, Morann wished Sunday would hurry up and come. The suspense was driving her to day-mares.

13

WHEN DAD CAME HOME THAT NIGHT, HE WAS ALL for the picnic. "Great idea," he said, unlacing his highcut field boots. "Just what I need. A good walk in the wilderness." He rubbed a foot jokingly. "And it's a chance to see Sarah."

Saturday morning, he didn't even consider the overnight fishing trip his friend Bob came round to suggest. "Flowers, not fish," he said flatly.

It was Bob who raised his eyebrows about the trip to the alpine meadows. "Just so it's a one-day jaunt," he said warningly.

"What did he mean, Dad?" Morann asked after Bob had left to raise another fishing partner.

"Oh, he's a bit off his rocker about keeping mining exploration out of that area until his wildlife club can present its brief at the hearings. If they can get it designated as a park, no one can touch it even if someone finds the Seven Dwarfs' diamonds. He's right, of course. Some of that land must be kept. I hope he succeeds, but it's going to be a hard fight."

Morann caught her breath. Maybe this was why Siem was "desperate." Perhaps the stlalakums knew that it would soon be too late to get that special gold out. Maybe it was now or never for working out some old stlalakum legend about the hidden treasure. She remembered that Kath had said the hearings were in October. So that was no worry. They could have the gold packed out of the mountains long before that. In fact, the time limit merely added an extra little tingle of excitement.

Her father was looking at her. "What's on your mind, Morann?"

"Oh." She shrugged. Then she sat bolt upright in the garden chair. "Dad. Dad, I'm planning a surprise for the picnic. And you've got to help me."

"Well, just so it doesn't involve baking a marble cake," he agreed. "That's not my kind of rock work."

"It just involves taking a few pictures and——"

"No problem. I'm planning on taking pictures.

"But these are special pictures. So will you please just do what I say when we get there?"

"Okay. I'll do just what you say when we get there. This is something pretty special, isn't it?"

"Oh, Dad! It's the most special thing that ever happened in my whole life."

"Then we've got to have pictures of it."

"Oh yes! We've got to have pictures of it." Pictures would give them exact information about the spot when they had to go back in later, maybe with a helicopter. For, once the tent was gone, it might be only too easy to get the little lakes and creeks mixed up. You were always hearing about gold that people couldn't find again when they went back in to get it.

Things continued to work out just too beautifully. And Morann was still crossing her fingers behind her back early Sunday morning when Dad finally said, "Looks like we're about ready to roll."

Gregory headed for the station wagon, dragging his tricycle.

"I don't think it's a place for tricycles," Dad objected.

"But Trikey wants to see the flowers."

"Maybe some other time. Okay?"

"Maybe after," Gregory agreed a little reluctantly. "Maybe he can even go by himself, after."

"After what?" Mom asked him.

"After we grow up. When he's a bus and I'm the driver."

"But——" Mom bit her lower lip and looked anxious.

Boy! Morann thought. Wait till she hears about Siem and the sky plume. She's really going to be worried. "Gregory, you and I are going to have a little talk one of these days. But there isn't time right now," Morann said, swooping up the tricycle and setting it behind the lilac bush. "Right now is Leg Day. Those alpine meadows are for legs and not for wheels. Okay?"

Somehow, she was feeling unusually on top of things. She had managed to set everything up without anybody suspecting anything.

"You really handled the weather well, Morann," her father said as he turned on the ignition.

"When I do things, I really do them," she agreed, stretching her arms wide to accept the loveliness of the summer morning.

It set the mood. Everyone made fun comments as they wound up along the mountain highway.

They slowed, passing the lake resort.

"Fish must be biting," Dad remarked with a nod towards the small boats sitting out in the lake. "Wish they'd bite those water skiers." The skiers' boats were churning up the quiet of the Sunday morning and laying a blue haze over the sparkle of the water.

He won't think that when we have water skis and a fast boat with a big outboard, Morann thought, hugging her plans to herself. Outboards

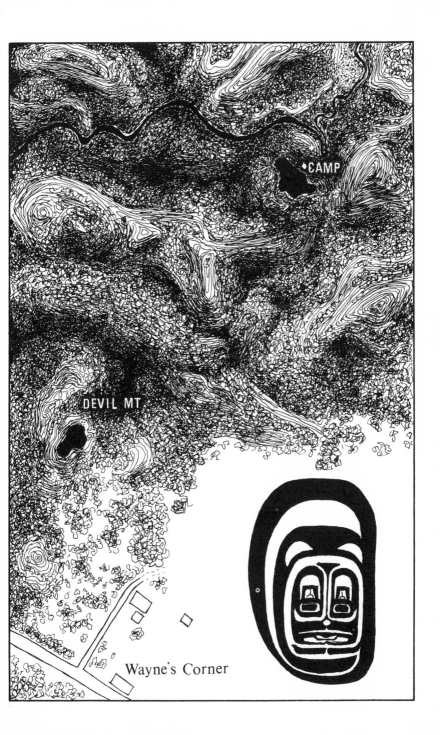

did make noise and smoke, of course; but that didn't bother you once you were in on the fun, too. Once Dad got up on water skis, he'd forget he had ever wanted everything quiet to suit the fishermen. She could just see him being quick and sure, the way he was on snow skis. Maybe she'd even be pretty good herself. Kath, of course. Kath would be quietly skillful. And Robin would start acting crazy. Morann could just see them all clamoring for their next turn, yet giving her an extra turn because, after all, she had bought the outboard. She wished to goodness they'd hurry up and get there.

Finally they did reach the gas station. They parked the car, divided up the stuff they were packing in for the surprise picnic, and walked towards the sign where the trail started.

Suddenly, at the edge of the wilderness, a reluctance came over Morann. For some reason she had a terrible urge not to go on. "Maybe we should give Gregory a snack before we hit the trail," she suggested, setting her cake pack down carefully.

"Good idea," Mom said; and she began to open up the handbasket with the orange juice and fig newtons. "It'll be a long hike for small legs."

"And after all, it is a Leg Day," Dad observed, dropping his heavy pack down, too, right on a patch of pea vine.

"It might hurt the flowers," Gregory cried out;

and he tugged the heavy pack off the peavine.

"So it might," his father agreed, moving the pack more. "I'd forgotten about frightening flowers."

"Dad!" Morann's voice expressed the surprise she felt. "Do you know about Cleve Backster's polygraph?"

"Sure. Bob gets *Wildlife* every month, so I get *Wildlife* secondhand every month. I know all about the polygraph. And I know all about the barley."

"What barley?"

"It was a university project. They ran an experiment, planting barley. They grew three plots in identical soil and gave them identical care except for one thing."

"What thing?"

"Well, I suppose you could call it emotional nourishment. All three plots got the same care. But the students running the project really poured the love onto one plot. They actively hated a second plot. And they treated the third plot with the detachment scientists are supposed to have if they want to get at the truth."

"And what happened?"

"Something that still floors me. The barley they loved sprouted up like Alice In Wonderland when she ate the right side of the mushroom. The barley they hated was definitely stunted. And the third plot grew exactly the way any agricultural scientist would have predicted it would grow with that kind of soil and water."

"So plants *can* think and feel!"

"But they've got nothing to think with or feel with," her father objected.

"That's exactly what Neil said."

"It must be vibrations," her father continued thoughtfully. "Maybe the kids are really on to something, talking about good vibes. Though the polygraph shows that what kids classify as good vibes—loud rock music—has the poor plants silently screaming at fifty paces."

"Vibrations or——" Morann clapped her hand over her mouth. She wasn't ready to tell them yet about the stlalakum sprites who might be doing the wincing.

"Or what?"

"Oh. You'll find out." She tossed her head knowingly.

"Little Miss Mystery?"

"Mmmmmmmm," she answered. But there was no tossing of the head this time. The full force of the facts had hit her. People could actually shrivel plants, or make them surge up, just by hating them or loving them. She had had her mind all the time on what plants might do to her, if she happened to hurt them. She hadn't really considered their terrible vulnerability when people moved in on them.

But Gregory changed the subject. "I told you.

I told you," he screeched, leaping up to watch a squirrel scamper up a tall fir. "He has comed. I told you."

"But maybe that isn't your squirrel," Morann countered, catching Mom's glance. "Maybe that's the . . . the Ogress squirrel." Wow! she thought. That's an improvement? But, with Gregory's eyes eagerly on her, she had to go on with a brief version of the tale of the clutching old Woman of the Woods and the tiny Chief's son.

"Is she still chasing him?" Gregory was wide-eyed with concern.

"Of course not," Mom told him. "It's just a silly old story, isn't it, Morann?" Her frown demanded agreement.

"It's just an old Indian story," Morann said. "Let's get on with the picnic!" she jumped up, eager now to go on. Dad's quiet acceptance of the newly-discovered relationship between plants and people had given her a resurgence of faith in her own uncanny adventure. Scientists would discover stlalakums, too, some day. They'd find out that Indians really had tuned in on the Wisdom of the Wild. Siem's expression flashed into her mind. *Wisdom of the Wild.* The words caught her fancy. Maybe the Wisdom of the Wild was the same thing as Neil's cosmic communications network. "Let's go!" she said, swooping up the cake pack. "See you, pea vine," she added, with a small bow. And it gave her a glow to think that her delight in their beauty could actually stimulate their growth. "Have a good day! Oh! Have a good day, everybody!"

All the way in along the trail to the campsite, she found herself sort of blessing the columbines and the mountain daisies. What she felt towards them actually mattered.

There was no one around the two tents.

"Oh, they'll turn up," Dad predicted lightly, "especially when they smell the goodies. And if they don't, there'll be all the more for us and the whiskyjacks." He indicated the two gray jays that had already joined the picnic.

"I love it. I love it. I love it," Gregory announced, tumbling in the grass by the small lake.

Morann heard Dad snap a picture.

"I love it . . . sitting down," Mom stipulated. She flopped down to take her shoes off. "It's turned out a really hot day."

Dad snapped another picture. But it wasn't of Mom, Morann discovered, when she turned to glance at him. His eyes were on something skyward. A small high cloud, stretching downward? She caught her breath and looked up. But there was no sky plume coming. There were just a few puffy white clouds against the blue, and a pair of big birds circling. "Eagles?" she asked, walking towards him.

"Hawks," her father told her. "The world's perfect gliders."

Round and round they soared in opposing spirals, rising above the mountain meadow. Up and up and up with never a wingbeat.

"Riding the vertical currents. Sensing the wing's perfect angle of attack." Dad's voice was filled with wonder. "Doing with ease what man can do very poorly even when he understands what is happening and when he has sophisticated instruments to help him. How do they know all about it?"

"The Wisdom of the Wild." This time she said it out loud.

"Where did you hear that expression?" her father asked, smiling at her.

"Oh, from a friend of mine." Siem was a friend, however reluctant. Siem had shown her where the treasure was . . . and now was the time.

"Dad." Morann's voice was eager.

"I know. Those pictures. One amateur photographer reporting for duty, Miss." But he took one long look back at the perfect gliders. "Man! To glide the way they glide! To soar with such pure skill! Wouldn't you like to be up there?"

"Well . . ." No. As a matter of fact, she wouldn't.

"There's so much we don't know yet."

Morann agreed. "There's so much we don't know yet." She might have to use those very words a little later. "Remember, Dad, you said it:

'There's so much we don't know yet.' You said it."

"I said it," he admitted.

"Let's hit the trail, Dad!" Suddenly, she couldn't bear to wait another minute. And maybe it would be better anyway if just she and Dad went. "Mom, Dad and I have a little project."

"Not before you eat?"

"We could take a pack of sandwiches, couldn't we, and eat with the gang later?"

"Me, too." Gregory joined the project.

"Well, at least have a drink first."

"But I've got my water canteen," Morann protested. "And we'll be following a clean creek." She accepted a good thick ham sandwich and a box of raisins. "We're going up that creek, just over that bump. Not far. See that you protect the cake from the whiskeyjacks, Mom!"

"Don't worry. I'm going to sit right here and protect everything from the whiskeyjacks and the bears. I'm not used to hiking."

"But you are used to fending off bears," Dad pointed out, teasingly.

"You're not tired, Morann?" Mom asked her.

"No siree."

"Neither me," cried Gregory.

"Okay men. Follow me!" Morann boomed it out to give herself courage. For all of a sudden, when it came right down to facing the facts, she didn't feel quite so certain. What if——?

What if nothing, she told herself firmly. The landmarks would be there.

And the treasure would be there, too.

14

THE STREAM WAS THERE ANYWAY. AND IT SEEMED TO have an enchantment Morann had not noticed before. Its perfectly transparent water splashed against the rocks, splintering into brilliant little sprays of crystal while fresh blue brook lobelia trembled with the excitement.

"I love it. I love it," Gregory cried out. "It's my creek."

"I believe it is," Morann agreed. "Listen!" She held her ear towards the gurgling water. "Gwuggelly Creek. Gwuggelly Creek.

"I can hear it. I can hear it," he screeched with pleasure.

Dad was taking pictures of them, slipping
quietly about to capture a variety of lovely back-
grounds: a flaming patch of magnificent Indian
paint brush, a stand of airy columbines with jew-
elled raiders hovering over, a high snow-capped
blue mountain rising behind the green trees, a
spectacular butterfly rocking on a slender green
stem. He was slung with two cameras: his
"good" camera for the color stills and his quick
polaroid, "so I can see what I'm getting."

Once when she glanced towards him, Morann
caught a tiny shimmer of pearly robes behind
him. "Siem!" But when she really looked, it had
vanished.

She felt the stlalakum presence hovering, however. She sensed a waitingness all around her.
And it was vaguely unnerving. What were they
all waiting for? Something—she didn't know

quite what—was nagging at her mind. Something about being worthy. You always had to be worthy on a quest.

She remembered the same sensed waitingness up on Devil Mountain, when the dark shadows were slipping down into the deep lake, and the little reptiles. Then they must have been waiting to see if she was brave. And the blackness of the silent night had been filled with eyes glowing from the forest and the luminous apparition swooping down without the least sound. All the old fears engulfed her.

"Dad." She just had to ask it. "Dad, do you think there could be a . . . a luminous bird in the real world?"

"The real world?" Her father looked at her strangely. "Wait a minute!" He smiled at her. "Bob was telling me something about a phosphorescent owl, if that's what you mean."

"Then it was real. I mean . . . that night in the mountains." He could think she meant the night she had camped with the others. "I was sure I saw something."

"You probably did. I understand it's rare, but it does happen. Something about a fungus that gets onto the feathers of owls who make their home in old, rotting buildings. You know, Morann, there usually is some simple explanation for anything that seems uncanny."

"That's what Sarah said, too." He could think

Sarah had said it about the owlish apparition and not about the loon's hauntingly wild call from a lonely lake. "Dad, I think we'd better push on." Suddenly she was too anxious to enjoy lingering by the lovely creek. The voices had said first test, before, at Devil Mountain. Would there be another? Her confidence had left her again. Would they find the landmarks after all? Would there be a treasure? And, most of all, would she do whatever you had to do to be worthy of it? They were waiting for her to do something. She could feel it all around her. "Dad. Let's go, eh?"

"You're the project boss," Dad agreed. "Come on, Greg! The boss says we have to push on."

"On up Gwuggelly Creek," Morann conceded, with a rush of fondness for her little brother. She took his warm hand, and found she was clinging to it.

"I got some beauties back there," her photographer told her. "I can see why Bob is so eager to save this place for posterity."

Morann thought she heard a motor. "Is that a jet?" she suggested, scanning the blue and white sky.

"Sounds more like something on the ground," her father answered. "Maybe it's one of those confounded trail bikes."

The way was a little steeper than she had expected from her aerial view. And Morann felt more and more anxious as she followed the creek upstream. Then she saw it. The mount of lupine, more blue than it had seemed in the silvering moonlight. "That's it," she cried out, her spirits rising. "I mean . . . that's another picture I want, Dad."

"A great picture," her father assured her. "That blue against all the green of the trees and the deeper blue of those background mountains and then the lighter blue of the sky again. Get into the picture. Okay?"

"Okay." Morann hurried over. She had never been this far up the creek on foot. But she had seen this mound from the sky plume. She spread her arms like the wings of a soaring eagle.

"I love it. I love it," Gregory cried, spreading his smaller wings behind hers.

"Great!" Dad called out. And he circled a thumb and forefinger in a gesture of triumph.

"Let's push on, eh?"

It was still steeper than she had expected. But she moved on up the slope in mounting excitement.

Then she saw the grove of trees. "That's it. That's it," she cried out jubilantly.

"Straight out of Disneyland," Dad cried. "Perfect miniature trees. A fantasy forest. Stand near them so we can see how tiny those trees are."

She hadn't realised they'd be so small. "A fantasy forest." Siem's forest, near Siem's hidden treasure. Morann had a strong feeling that

the Noble One was hovering near her. There was something strange about all this, something more than letting her have the treasure. She felt oddly alien, oddly big and clumsy, standing by Siem's forest. Every tree was so small, yet so utterly perfect. Was it too perfect to be real? Would it vanish the way Siem did, because, in some way, she was unworthy of it?

"Hold it!" Dad cried out. "Morann, you have a great eye for pictures."

"Just you wait, Dad!" She crossed her fingers.

Next they would come upon the rock outcropping in its bank of golden flowers. Now she knew it would be there. It would be. "Come on, men!" she commanded. "Get your lens set for pure gold!"

"Listen!" said Gregory. "I think I hear something."

It was the snarl of an engine, louder now and coming closer.

"Well," Dad said, shrugging, "I guess we don't own the place. But they say we're going to be stone deaf by year 2000 because of all these rackets. Why can't the kids walk in?"

Morann scarcely heard him. Intent now on her quest, she almost held her breath; she almost tiptoed; she almost peeped ahead through her fingers. It would be there. It would be there, just as she remembered from her trip in the sky plume.

"There it is," she murmured, almost reverently.

There was the rock outcropping in its bank of golden flowers. Above the rock, the golden bloom was matted, like moss touched by Midas. Below it, the flowers were tall enough to have bowed to Siem as the sky plume had passed over. And they all seemed to gather in the sun's light, concentrating the bright rays into a glow of enchantment.

"Lens set for pure gold," her father reported. "Are the actors all ready? Lights! Camera! Action!"

He got far more action than Morann had intended. For, suddenly roaring up, shattering her golden moment, a trail bike growled towards them from behind a grove of small trees.

"Joe!" Morann was aghast to see him, right now.

"Hi!" he called, coming at them with a flourish. Then he skillfully swerved and stopped dead in a marginal patch of fragile golden flowers.

Gregory screeched at him.

"Gregory. Gregory," Morann soothed her little brother. "Joe won't hurt you."

"He's scaring the flowers." Gregory was still screeching, his arms widely defensive as though he were protecting the whole bank of flowers.

Joe stood there by his bike, red-faced and repentent. "Gosh, Morann, I . . . I just told you I'd give you the first ride when I got my trail bike." He looked desperately contrite. "Gosh, Gregory, I

· 177 ·

sure didn't mean to scare your flowers." He pushed his bike off the small patch and tried to straighten a broken blossom. "Here, I'll give you a candy bar."

"I don't want a candy bar. I don't want the flowers hurted."

"Joe won't hurt them again," Morann soothed him. "He didn't know about flowers. Joe, you haven't heard about the polygraph, have you?"

"Well, you will now," Dad informed him, thumping one sweaty shoulder. "And you'll hear about the barley."

"So you might as well sit down," Morann said in a very small voice. Joe's arrival seemed positively timed to stop her, at the moment of her triumph.

"Sure thing." Joe was eager to do anything that might help to square things.

Morann told him about the plants. And she felt as if she were carefully listening to her own words, searching for some clue.

"Gosh!" Joe exclaimed when she had finished. "I sure didn't know that, or I'd never have brought the bike in here." He bent eagerly towards the polaroid snaps Dad was laying out in order on a small patch of flat grass. Then he went red to the roots of his hair as he picked up the last one, the one of Gregory fiercely defending his flowers against the onrushing monster.

"A little boy's treasure," Dad said softly, as

though titling the picture.

"Treasure." Morann was stunned. Treasure? Treasure! She had equated treasure with gold. Now understanding flooded through her. This was Siem's treasure. This was why the Keeper of the Stlalakum Wild was desperate to enlist people. This was the reason for the gesture of impatience every time Morann had said "gold." How could she ever have been stupid enough to imagine that Siem would help her to dig up the earth? To destroy even one lovely spot in the great Stlalakum Wild?

There wasn't any gold here.

Her rainbow collapsed like the rainbow in a soaring soap bubble.

There wasn't any gold here. She wasn't going to be important, with her name in the paper. She wasn't going to be the much-admired giver of gifts to the family.

"You working up a brief for the hearings in October?" Joe asked her father.

"Well . . ." Dad looked questioningly at Morann.

"Yeah." She jumped at the idea. It would save the situation. Make her not look quite the fool she was. "Yeah. You know. Sort of . . . you know. A children's crusade," Morann ad-libbed.

"So that's what you had in mind?" Dad looked delighted. "I'm proud of you, Morann. And I'm impressed, too. You certainly had it mapped out."

He was sorting through the pictures. "Wait until I get those good shots developed for you! This'll be a brief to knock their eyes out. We'll beat old Bob at his own game!"

Morann cringed inside. The only time anybody admired her was when she didn't rate admiration, when there wasn't much satisfaction in getting it.

They heard familiar "Yoo-hoos."

"Coming! her father sang out. "You even had it timed right. Those girls sniffed the goodies. So we're ready for the celebration." He swooped up Gregory, hoisted him up onto his shoulders, and began to gallop downstream.

"I'm sure sorry about this," Joe said, misunderstanding Morann's misery. He looked so contrite and so clumsy she could have wept for him.

Or maybe it's me I could weep for, she thought. The way things always turned out! After all her golden dreams, she was right back where she started. Only now they thought she was kookie as well as stupid and showoff.

"Well, let's face the food, Joe." She meant, "Let's face the family." And she developed just a touch of a swagger as she led the way downstream.

"Hi!" Robin boomed out in welcome at the campsite. "We thought you had gone off for a ride in the sky plume."

"Hi," Kath said more briskly. And she drew Morann aside. "Look!" she started right in. "I caught Mom saying 'When Morann got home Friday' didn't I?"

"Probably. You have ears like a bugged room."

"Well." Kath flipped her red notebook open. "You left here Thursday morning."

"Right," said Morann. "I left here Thursday morning."

"So?" All Kath demanded was a nice sensible explanation.

"So you're going to worry Mom."

Kath positively snorted. "*I'm* going to worry Mom? Huh!"

"Well. Are you?" Morann looked challengingly up at the tallest, oldest, darkest, skinniest, and bossiest of the Fenn girls.

"I'll talk to you later, Morann."

Right now Dad was talking. ". . . and wait till you hear what Morann has been planning. Come on! Tell them, young lady."

"You tell them, Dad, will you?" What Siem had been planning. Siem had probably even sent Joe roaring in to make her understand about the treasure. How could she have been so stupid? How could she have so fixed her mind on gold that she didn't even understand about the real nature of the treasure until it was almost too late? But gold was like that. Kind of blinding.

She noticed that Kath was squealing. "A brief's a marvellous idea. We can list the birds and flowers. Add a section on the Indian legends." She

· 181 ·

opened her notebook and began her swift jottings. Kath was off and away, running; she'd take the whole thing over. Siem would have the most efficient "body" in the country saving the great Stlalakum Wild.

"A surprise picnic's an even more marvellous idea," Robin declared, piling food on her paper plate.

Neil and Sarah were almost silent.

Suddenly, Morann couldn't bear it. Watching her chance, she slipped away from the picnic. She found refuge up the creek near the mound of blue lupines. If the voices came back, let them! If a sasquatch carried her off, he'd bring her back soon enough.

A glint caught her eye, a glint in the creek bed.

Morann plunged her arm in and picked up a nugget.

"A gold nugget!" She whispered in pure awe.

There was gold in the rock, then; the river betrayed it. This was the way every gold rush had started! Someone picked up a nugget washed out of the rock by the water.

She caught a shimmer of pearl across the creek. "Siem!"

The Noble One stayed silent, motionless as the mountains. And the world seemed to be waiting, waiting, waiting. The whole world of the Stlalakum Wild.

Morann caught her breath. They were all waiting for her.

She closed her hand around the nugget. Her fortune was in her fingers, for the nugget was merely a token of the wealth that was waiting. She could merely show the nugget and——

And machinery would move in. Fragile flowers would be trampled in the rush to the river. Slag heaps would pile up, grey and ugly. Greedy people would rush in, tearing up the whole region. Snarling engines would roar through it.

Yet . . . the gifts for the family.

"I don't want a candy bar." she could hear Gregory now. "I don't want the flowers hurted."

Siem's voice from across the creek was as clear and bright as the running water. "Everything and everybody has a potential for good or for harm, Morann. You must make your own decision."

She must make her own decision, while the lovely world waited for its doom, for its destruction. She had more power than she wanted.

"Hey! Morann!" Neil was coming towards her. "I got worried about you. You do some pretty weird things these days."

"Right. I do. I do some pretty weird things these days." Morann slipped the gold nugget swiftly into her pocket and zippered it up tight. She was not going to be rich. Not going to be important. She was going to be something better. She was going to be worthy of the beauty the world had built up. And for no reason that she knew, she turned a cartwheel.

"What's with you?" Neil asked her.

"The whole world's with me." Morann spread her arms wide. She could feel it *with* her. The whole lovely natural world of the great Stlalakum Wild. Then her hand covered her pocket, as though to protect something precious.

"You found something," Neil accused her.

"Of course I found something. People off on a quest always find something, don't they? I found——" What could she say she had found? "Spirit power." Now where did that idea come from? she wondered. But it was true, wasn't it? If loving a plot of barley could make it grow better, then love for living things was power, wasn't it? Like the sun's power. It was the power of your potential for good or evil. The power to make things grow, or to shrivel them.

"Look," Neil reminded her. "They'll be getting anxious."

"And we've got a project to work on, right?" She'd go flat out on that brief now—like Kath—and save the meadows. "Race you," she told Neil, taking off like a squirrel.

She burst into camp laughing.

It was Sarah who drew Morann aside this time.

"Morann. I've been studying these pictures. Did you notice this cloud formation?" She held up the last picture.

"The sky plume." Morann gasped.

Sarah looked at her, incredulous.

"I'll tell you about it some day." She turned to go off, but Sarah grabbed her by the shoulders. "Morann, I have a feeling that I should really have listened to you the other day.

"Oh, pooh," Morann scoffed lightly.

"No, I mean it, Morann! You're positively glowing. Something wonderful has happened to you."

"Something wonderful," Morann admitted. She grinned and whispered in her aunt's ear. "Something wonderful and stlalakum."

"You mean . . . really? Something uncanny really happened?"

"Yes. But as you said, 'There's always a simple explanation for anything that seems uncanny.' "

Relief showed in Sarah's face. "So there is a simple explanation?"

"A very simple explanation. *There's an awful lot we don't know yet.*"

Sarah looked astonished, and suddenly eager. "Morann, you're amazing."

"Well, it's nice to be something," Morann told her. And this time there was no edge of resentment in her voice, no loudness. It *was* nice to be something. A fern's friend. A daisy's defender. A really welcome wanderer in the great Stlalakum

Wild. The living, breathing, mysterious Stlalakum Wild. "See you next summer," she added softly.

"You will see me next summer." Sarah made it a promise.